# THE LONG MARCH OF BASIC TRUST

THE GERMAN LIST

# ALEXANDER KLUGE

## THE LONG MARCH OF BASIC TRUST

CHRONICLE OF EMOTIONS: NOTEBOOK 2

TRANSLATED BY ALEXANDER BOOTH

LONDON NEW YORK CALCUTTA

This publication has been supported by
a grant from the Goethe-Institut India.

Parts of this text have previously appeared in other translations.
The present edition, however, is a complete translation
rendered in its entirety by the current translator.

Seagull Books, 2025

Published in German as *Der lange Marsch des Urvertrauens*
in *Chronik der Gefühle*, Band II
© Suhrkamp Verlag, Frankurt am Main, 2000
All rights reserved by and controlled through Suhrkamp Verlag Berlin

First published in English translation by Seagull Books, 2025

English translation © Alexander Kluge Stiftung, 2025

ISBN 978 1 80309 547 9

British Library Cataloguing-in-Publication Data
A catalogue record for this book is available from the British Library

Typeset by Seagull Books, Calcutta, India

## CONTENTS

| | |
|---|---|
| The Spanish Sentry | 3 |
| The Pedagogue of Klopau | 3 |
| Those Who Hope Die Singing | 7 |
| Arrival of Sunday's Child | 11 |
| The Long March of Basic Trust | 13 |
| The Expression 'Basic Trust' | 14 |
| Cooperative Behaviour | 15 |
| Back to Basic Trust | 16 |
| Basic Trust and Basic Fear | 16 |
| Distrust towards Reality | 18 |
| On the Deep Sleep of the Spirit | 19 |
| Waking Sleep of Whales and Dolphins | 22 |
| Undoing a Crime by Means of Cooperation | 24 |
| A Saturday in October 1929 | 35 |
| The Man without Qualities | 37 |
| They Did Not Come to Any Conclusion | 40 |
| Wanderer by Night | 42 |
| Executing an Elephant | 43 |
| The Emperor of My Trust | 45 |
| Star Wars | 46 |
| Clear Moscow Evenings, When the Northwest Wind Blows | 47 |
| Galina Starovoitova | 49 |
| 20 Billion Years Before Christ | 52 |

| | |
|---|---|
| More Animals on Earth than Stars in the Milky Way | 60 |
| The Confidence of Caged Cows | 64 |
| Negligence in War, Nuclear Power and the Death Penalty | 66 |
| The Blind and the Inexperienced | 68 |
| Encounter with the Unknown | 70 |
| The Waltz of the Generals | 77 |
| A 570-Million-Year-Old Cloak of Invisibility | 81 |
| Robinson in Russia | 84 |
| The Quantum Vacuum, a Poetic Metaphor | 86 |
| My Paternal Ancestors | 88 |
| A Complicated Generational Sequence | 88 |
| Thinking About One's Own Children in 1908 | 90 |
| How the War Was Lost | 92 |
| The Inventor of Infiltration Tactics | 93 |
| '. . . like a multitude of soft whistles . . .' | 94 |
| A Forgotten Weapon | 96 |
| The Fifth Art of Forgetting | 97 |
| The Power of Fate | 100 |
| Extreme Dwarves | 108 |
| Devils Have a Waiting Period | 116 |
| The Underwater Artist | 122 |
| Modern Humankind | 123 |
| Slave Water | 125 |
| A Lift into the Oceanic Depths | 126 |
| Heiner Müller and Project Spring Water | 128 |

*Sketches of time periods longer than a single lifespan: the stars, aeons, generations.*

*We who are left over from the past carry something within ourselves without which we would have never survived: BASIC TRUST. Every living being receives their share at birth.*

*'Those who hope die singing.'*

## THE SPANISH SENTRY

In an army barracks in Spain lay a pile of straw. A sentry was placed before it. The straw mouldered, collapsed into a tiny pile. Not having been recalled, the sentry continued to stand there for months.

## THE PEDAGOGUE OF KLOPAU

Friedrich Nietzsche (via Josefine Nauckhoff): 'That there are books so valuable and regal that entire generations of scholars are well employed when, through their efforts, these books are preserved in a pure and intelligible state—philology exists to reinforce this faith again and again.'

In thousands of Latin schools across Germany in the years 1943/44, young people came of age in the shadow of the great philologist F. A. Wolf. Due to a misshapen leg, teaching candidate Dr Friedrich Rühl could not serve his country with a weapon. He was passionate about the teaching profession, which he had been preparing for since 1939. He fervently believed in children's ability to learn, their good will, their propensity for *Bildung*, that is, general education and self-cultivation, which is what decides the future. His academic teachers were Martini and Heidorn in Berlin; he believed in individualized education.

During Rühl's traineeship, an intelligent Latin student died while completing a giant, under the supervision of the sports teacher; Rühl and another trainee were involved in the already hopeless attempt at finding medical help.

Following his second state exam in autumn 1944, assessor Dr Rühl was sent fairly quickly to Klopau, in West Prussia. He arrived there on 10 January. On 12 January, Russian troops pushed from their bridgeheads on the Vistula into Poland. Workers were needed to help build a new frontline. Before his lessons at the Klopauer Gymnasium could even begin in proper fashion, assessor Rühl, hastily promoted to the position of superintendent, had to put together a group of pupils fit for military service and entrenchment, and set them marching into the hinterland. Around Graudenz, they dug holes from which they could attack tanks (these were known as Panzerlöcher). The students quickly learnt how to dig. Just a little while later, Russian tanks were close by. Surprised while at work, 12 students died. At that point, Dr Rühl was entrusted with provisional school supervision throughout the district of Klopau.

Practically speaking, in only 12 weeks, Rühl went from assessor to superintendent. The night following the tank attack on 18 January, the remaining 18 students attempted to carry a wounded colleague to Wilby, where there was supposed to be a field hospital. Even before getting there, the students received Panzerfäuste and assault rifles. Near the intersection by Wiltrusch-Lengsby, at their teacher's suggestion, they attempted to ward off a Russian tank. A group of four students, together with their one-footed teacher, remained unseen; the rest died. Rühl did everything he could to get at least those four back to the territory of the Reich. On the heels of the retreating 9th Army through the Spree Forest southeast of Berlin, a student trying to get hold of a piece of meat was lost to artillery fire. Following a motorized convoy, the teacher and three pupils reached Berlin and reported to the Reich and Prussian ministries of culture. The pupils were transferred to a student-collection centre in Spandau-West.

After the war, Rühl shied away from a return to the teaching profession. During the days of the black market, he opened a stamp exchange. In 1948, he changed professions once again and became a real-estate agent.

Film stills from *Der Pädagoge von Klopau* (The Pedagogue of Klopau). A sequence from *Lehrer im Wandel* (Teachers in Transformation), 1963.

## THOSE WHO HOPE DIE SINGING

This is the story of Antoine Billot. He was involved in the catastrophe of Arles. Hundreds of dead overnight due to the breaking of a dam. By the time the boat-bound soldiers managed to free Billot from the tree to which he was clinging, he was already unconscious from hunger and cold.

In 1939, together with four other trackmen, he found himself underneath a locomotive, for something with the warning system had gone wrong. The train crew, who were only able to bring the express train to a halt a few metres past the scene of the accident, a blind bend, were replaced in the next town. Damages to the locomotive were few. Our man was not given immediate medical attention as he had been lumped in with the rest of the dead; later, he managed to pull himself together.

On another day, a concrete ceiling collapsed, and seven women in the room, who were peeling potatoes for a company, were killed. He was the only man there. At the time of the accident, he was standing in the doorway and was therefore only seriously injured, not killed; all the same, doctors doubted whether he would recover. The story made the papers.

During the war, he was flown back to the interior of the country where he'd been injured. When one of the ambulance plane's engines stopped working and the aircraft lost altitude, the ground crew gave the order to drop the gravely wounded. He was one of them. Out he went. As there was a shortage of parachutes, no one would have expected to hear anything more from him. But he had a double dose of luck: he not only survived his fall but was also nursed back to health on the farm where he came to ground. In the end, this also kept him from being imprisoned and used as forced labour in Germany. After victory, he made the foolish decision to make his way home to the south of France. In Nîmes, he ended up among the arrested militia members who were driven into the stadium and machine-gunned. Either by mistake or because he'd actually had something to do with the militia. He lay there, shot, covered by a few corpses that fell on top of him; then, as he used to say, he was dragged off like a dead bull. Nevertheless, later, once again, he managed to get away.

He was freed from military duty in Algiers. He also stopped accepting work in companies whose accident rate was above 1.2 per cent per year. It just so happened that, one day, watching a football match in the stadium of a small town in the south of France in the golden evening sun, the stands filled to capacity, there was a sudden torrential downpour, the whole sky was a single dam of water, and thousands of onlookers rushed to the exits out of fear of getting wet. Twenty people were left lying there, some dead, some seriously wounded. The in-the-meantime 40-year-old Billot—already close to the exit—belonged to the considerably blessed, and once again managed to evade death. The injury from which he had to recover, compounded by a liver ailment and mild blood poisoning due to improper treatment in the district hospital, prevented him from taking part in the Suez adventure, which, at the time, no one knew would end dangerously. The man was thankful.

Film stills from *Wer immer hofft, stirbt singend* (Those Who Hope Die Singing). James Ensor & Alexander Kluge: Dark Centuries / Siècles noirs: 1492, 1942, 2042. Fondation Vincent van Gogh, Arles, 2018.

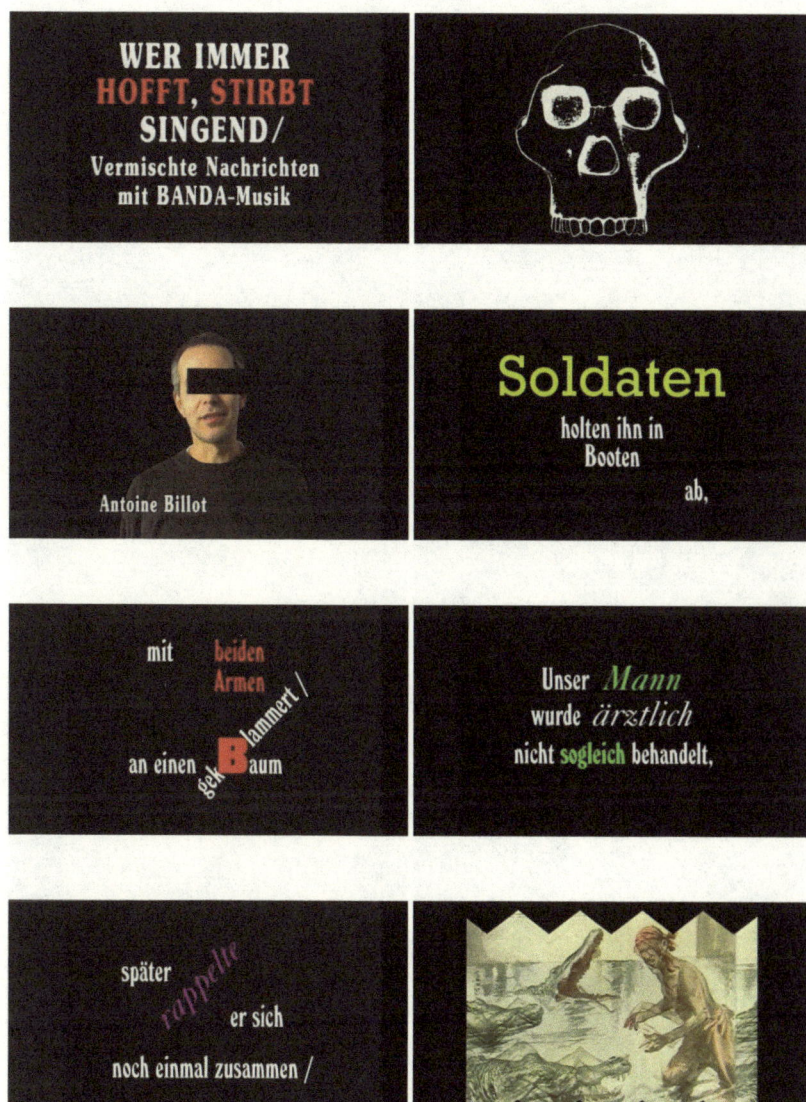

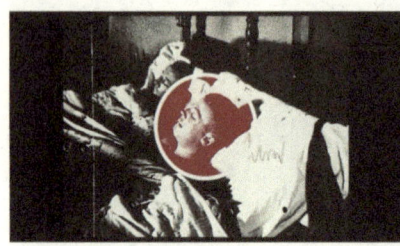

Er lag *angeschossen*, *verdeckt* von einigen Toten,

und wurde, wie er später erzählte, wie ein *toter Stier*, abgeschleppt /

*Der Mann war dankbar /*

## ARRIVAL OF SUNDAY'S CHILD

Things went on until three in the morning. The child, arriving in the world at 11.55 p.m., bathed, photographed, placed in the young mother's arms, *still counts as a Sunday child.*

At this point, the servant girls are in their rooms. All the drunk well-wishers, sunk in the sofas or lying across the salon floors, are fast asleep. The day following the excitement is a Monday. The girls clean up the remains of the feast. The head doctor is already in his office. Patients are coming up the stairs to the waiting room. The female doctor is asleep.

The child in the room next to the female doctor has been 'forgotten' for a few hours. Although all carry the 'news of the happy event' in their excited hearts, the basket with the child has been put away and it will be noon before anyone thinks to ask about the new arrival's regularities.

First, the flowers in the winter garden need to be stowed away. Stocks from the pantry brought to the cleaning woman's family. They are considered to have been 'used yesterday'.

The young doctor can hardly believe that, at all of 24, she has managed a birth. She's got earplugs in, is fast asleep. Were visitors not expected to come to offer congratulations for the 'Sunday child' during the afternoon, you could easily forget that piece of meat in the basket, even if it screamed.

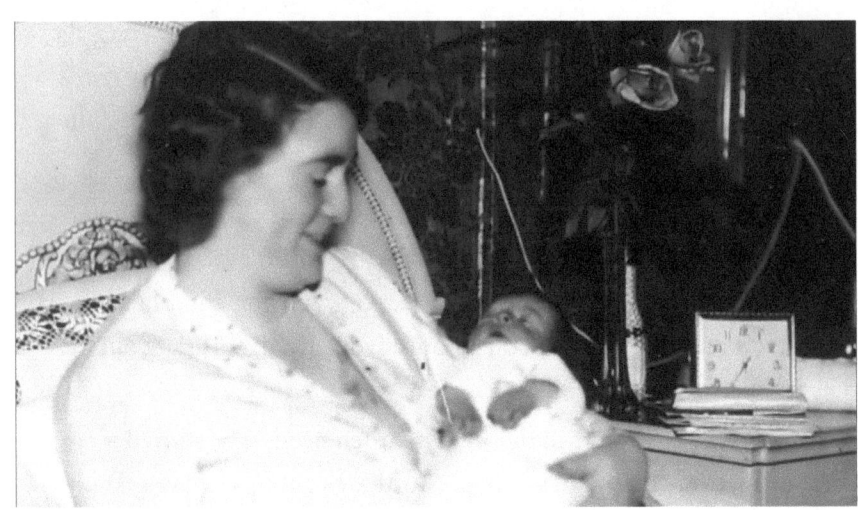

FIGURE 1. Next to my mother. Around 95 minutes after my birth. The clock on the nightstand shows a little after 1.30 a.m. Wrapped up nice and warm. Friendly eyes all around. Presumably, I have not yet begun to perceive them. Everything up close. Presumably, I am not 'thinking' about anything. My bowels are painstakingly learning to 'work'. My entire system is undergoing conversion. The beginning of my long march.

## THE LONG MARCH OF BASIC TRUST

There is a fundamental mistake to which all living creatures that have found their way to us through evolution—in other words, that have survived—cling: basic trust. For evolution, this mistake seems to be an advantage. After birth, people immediately believe—and we can assume that animals do too—that the world means well. A complete mistake. Marx would say: 'A necessary false consciousness.' The world does not mean well.

And yet we live from this trust. This is a treasure which, until the end of our lives, none of us gives up too easily. Our ability to envision horizons is based on this. It is what Nietzsche means when he is doubtful about our being truth-seeking creatures and says that we are 'immersed in illusions' instead. And without any doubt we spin cocoons about ourselves which warm us on the inside.

*Thomas Combrink*

## THE EXPRESSION 'BASIC TRUST'

The expression 'basic trust' goes back to the German American psychoanalyst Erik H. Erikson, born 1902, died 1994; his book *Childhood and Society* deals with the concept. It has to do with the first months of a person's life, when practised habits together with a caregiver's affection create lasting confidence. For Erikson, the earliest evidence of trust in reality is in the smooth sequence of bodily processes—the feeding, digestion and sleep of the newly born human running without a hitch. The child's first feat of abstraction concerns its ability to allow its mother out of its field of vision. The child continues to carry its closest caregiver in its heart because it can rely on ingrained habits, on the spontaneous elimination of aversion. Regarding trust, Niklas Luhmann speaks of 'overdrawn information'. This is the opposite of control. 'Trust is based on illusion. In reality, there is not as much information as you need to be able to act with confidence. The person acting deliberately ignores the lack of information,' Luhmann writes.

## COOPERATIVE BEHAVIOUR

Following the air raid of 11 February 1943, the charred remains of a human being were found in a building in Blaubach. One of the occupants maintained it was her husband. Another woman from the same building came forward to say that her husband had been in that bombed-out cellar too; in fact, the two had probably been sitting next to each other. Which meant that they had to be the bodily remains of the second woman's husband as well. She too would like to be able to visit a grave. The occupant who had returned to the rubble first suggested they share the charred man's odds and ends.

---

By the time the young Franziska Ziegler—who at the beginning of the attack had sought out a public bunker—returned, all that was left of the building was the left-hand firewall. Her 18-year-old sister joined her. Martha and Viktor Ziegler were standing up to their chests in the rubble against the wall. When the girls called their father, his head fell forward. The basement ceiling, a square piece of concrete, hung from a single iron bracket. They went and found petroleum and attempted to burn the dead. 'If we don't do it, the rats will.' They had to.

## BACK TO BASIC TRUST

If I desire to be a good parent, I don't really want my child to fly down the stairs. But how else will it learn?

In Halberstadt, I learnt to the metre how to do harm to one's bones. In Halberstadt, where I was born, as each one of us is born somewhere. But from my first days and experiences I am now going to make a jump. I am thirteen. I am a gauge, like all human beings, an echo chamber, making its way through the world and trying to write down and measure everything. A bat, in other words.

## BASIC TRUST AND BASIC FEAR

I do not trust basic fear, as it is, so to speak, a kind of inverted form of basic trust, a basic trust that has been disappointed. And as far as emancipation is concerned, self-consciousness, fear is a very poor counsellor. There is a certain politics of balance to self-consciousness. For example: Siegfried destroys everything due to excessive self-consciousness, he has no equanimity, he doesn't listen to anyone or anything beyond the birds in the forest, he upsets the whole court of Burgundy and works for its downfall; a case of self-consciousness flying solo, as it were. I would place much more trust in quieter forms in which self-consciousness can unite with another self-consciousness in a quasi-musical way, in which the two halves of our brain can correspond with each other as well. There is something paralysing about fear. Incidentally, I do not believe that there is such thing as a basic primal fear—it is not primal, it is always a matter of experience.

If I know that I sprained my arm when I flew down the stairs as a child, I can metaphorically fly down the stairs more often in my future life. Fear is translatable. There is a hysterical fear that is necessary in any nervousness. We are simply not alert without a certain amount of hysteria. There is certainly a fear of depth, something that the Romans call *numen*, which can also contribute the fear of god. People need a certain quantity of it, like a vaccination. It's like a garment, like armour. Under certain circumstances it may protect, but it doesn't motivate, it isn't productive. To live, we need a more powerful motive than fear.

Here we come into a rather complex form of alchemy, because we human beings require everything. An order in Napoleon's army was *jaccia feroce!*, ferocious face—his soldiers were to adopt faces absent of fear. No superior or partisan leader can control their soldiers if they forbid fear. It must be allowed to live. Put another way: *All of the sensations we have can be described as the ability to discriminate.* The Enlightenment philosophers in France were known as *amis d'analyse*, friends of analysis, friends of the ability to discriminate. This is an originally enlightened point of view. The mass production of this ability to discriminate is what connects us as human beings, and this includes the sphere of fear too. Hearing stories is a great source of satisfaction, as is talking confidentially and sharing our fears. Fears diminish, shared fear is less dangerous, and a relationship of trust develops. Being able to admit what you are afraid of is proof of trust. Being able to tell someone about your weakness—fear is often weakness in this sense—and not being criticized for it creates trust. The motive is trust, not fear. What sets things in motion is the motive, the supply, the fuel, so to speak.

## DISTRUST TOWARDS REALITY

I have a certain mistrust towards reality. This has to do with my experiences in Halberstadt. *I believe that the most extreme ideology that exists is the one that takes reality to be real.*

FIGURE 2. My mother Alice 'as Madame Butterfly' and I, six months old. Made with the 'virtual camera' known as Stable Diffusion.

## ON THE DEEP SLEEP OF THE SPIRIT

The researcher Ch. L. Lymen was interested, like everyone else, in immortality, or at least the extension of his productive life. He did not particularly care for this life, but he didn't want to give it away lightly or too soon because his mental makeup consisted in part of the oft-repeated couplet:

Something beautiful may come of this, of worth,
So grant me, please, one moment more on earth.

Lymen had made an interesting observation concerning LEBANESE BATS. They live considerably longer than their small size would suggest. This, it's said, could have something to do with hibernation.

Unfortunately, these bats are not suitable for research. They cannot be bred in captivity. They have a lifespan of 20 to 30 years. Since they must be caught for us to study them, we don't know anything about their history or how old they are. And if, labelled and fitted with a transmitter, they are released after captivity, they die.

For this reason, Turkish hamsters are used instead. Of the 288 lab animals, half were kept at a daily temperature of 25° C. The rest could sink into hibernation from November to April with temperatures of around −5° C. There was a clear correlation between hibernation and length of life. The best sleepers (hibernators) lived 200 days longer than those who enjoyed their permanent summer.[1]

Does this tell us anything about human breeding? The creation of future generations? These questions were supposed to secure funds from NASA. The selection procedure for Earth emigrants (whether to the greenhouses of Mars or one of Jupiter's habitable

---

1 R. R. Kohn, *Principles of Mammalian Aging*, 1978: Active life in the cold contains life-shortening stress. This is overcome by hibernation. Every animal is equipped with a supply of metabolic activity at birth. Once these reserves are exhausted, the animal dies.

moons) had nothing to do with the existence of humanity as it is, but with the breeding of a higher species.[2] From a genetic-engineering standpoint, this had already been attempted via illegal experiments. However, only partial aspects or shifts in human grievances were ever achieved. Moreover, unpredictability remained over long periods of time. Under unknown new conditions, a change in the 13th generation could unleash hell or bring happiness.[3]

A subjective approach, on the other hand, Lymen says, would be much simpler, i.e. in the hardware of which the *developed* human being consists. The power of the soul—in other words, its initial endowment of basic trust, the degree of exertion it expends—can be controlled by a DEEP SLEEP OF THE SPIRIT. This, Lymen continues, can even be done with open eyes, even while performing everyday tasks, it is something like a moment of ABSENCE. How is this achieved? Through sensitization to the cold current in the world. The soul shivers. It prepares itself to sleep for hundreds of years. In order to then awaken and unleash its ORIGINAL POWER. The 'lifelong vibration of basic trust' becomes concern or attentiveness. In the trance of 'hibernation', such vibration is paused. This state should not, however, be confused with DISPERSION, DIVERSION or DISSOLUTION. It is 'unconcerned wakefulness', a kind of 'absence'. Such a 'light sense' (supported by drugs, but triggered by sensitivity to coldness of the soul as it objectively arises

---

2 Cost of transporting a human together with their environment to Mars or to the neighbourhood of a giant planet: 20 million USD; this includes an engineering discount of 80 per cent of current prices. The subject value must therefore be adjusted to the real value. There is no point in taking lay people there.

3 Similar to a Sigmund or Siegfried planned into the future by God, who in the earthly context, i.e. as soon as he leaves the abstract forest or the possibility form, causes all-round mischief. A powerful force in the wrong context.

in the form of UNHAPPY HUMANITY and the CREATURE'S INDIFFERENCE TOWARDS NATURE AND THE COSMOS) corresponds to the 'hibernation' of the higher animals in the subjective world.[4] But, in fact, fish and most likely even unicellular organisms 'sleep'.

One advantage of this approach, Lymen writes,[5] lies in the rehabilitation of educational research. On the basis of a lifespan of 80 to 90 years (with a subsequent generation break, no generation really continues the work of the previous one), the *eruditio hominis* (this and not the gift of reason is what constitutes the *homo novus*) is comparable to a surface alloy that is too thin. A spaceship of this kind would come apart. An innovative re-positioning of self-cultivation, basic trust and waking hours, however, could change this. Lymen was hoping to receive a response to his research proposal from NASA by Advent. Why didn't the project he was so passionate about relate to 'a life on earth'? Because life on earth, he replied, does not allow for beauty. Not even with the individual's somewhat longer stay thanks to our current spare-parts system. The chance to fashion the earth into something more beautiful, Lymen maintains, lies in the fact that inside humans or other transportable creatures the more beautiful resides at a hostile distance. This is how the principle of hibernation functioned in the Hyperboreans (a rather advanced people brought to their end by the Stone Age and its invasions), 'coming in from the cold'. Lymen is placing all his hopes on exodus.

---

4 This, Lymen says, is the point of the 'light sense' attributed to the Valkyrie Brünnhilde in Richard Wagner by her maker Wotan. This spirit, which carries future-forward messages for the salvation of humanity and the gods, also 'sleeps' for centuries, perhaps even for more than a thousand years.

5 We are only at the beginnings of sleep research.

## WAKING SLEEP OF WHALES AND DOLPHINS

Neurobiologist Martin Korte of Braunschweig tells me that marine mammals cannot afford to sleep as we humans and land-based animals do. They must breathe in a foreign element. They must regulate their buoyancy even when asleep. And so, Korte says, they regulate their equilibrium (= what we call *sleep*) alternately with the left or right hemisphere of their brains; the one that is not asleep stays awake.

> 'Something beautiful may come of this, of worth,
> So grant me, please, one moment more on earth.'

# UNDOING OF A CRIME THROUGH MUTUAL COOPERATION

### I

Ingrid Fahle, engineer of the evening hour. She turns on the light, lets the client in, hands him a condom. The client undresses. She peels off her clothing. With an engineer's grip, she encloses her client's testicles, nonchalant. She is skilful. She frees her client from the tight condom. Lays him down on the massage table and makes herself at home. The anticipation is supposed to last. She massages his ankles, kneecaps, calves. She moves up to his chest.

Her client relaxes. Without uttering a word, he invites her to handle his neck a little more roughly. She strangles him a bit. She charges 180 marks. The tip of this assessor's sweeper is like a miniature Brussels sprout, but taut at the end, and reveals a male slit from which semen will come later on. She knows there'll be no more to expect after that—she diverts his attention. An old issue of *STERN*. The client looks at the pictures.

### II

She blends into the 5 o'clock–Friday wave of people bustling down Kaiserstraße to the train station. Straining her circulatory system does her good, she crosses Moselstraße, Taunusstraße, Niddastraße. She takes the four stairs up to her private flat. Undoes the lock. Exhausted from the workweek, she opens the front door, intends to make herself a tea; she sees the Yugoslavian lying in the heavy lounge chair, head encrusted with blood, sideways on the backrest.

She's known this Yugoslavian for several weeks now. 'On a business trip from Zagreb to Brussels, supposed to buy a dishwasher for my hotel.' 'I wanted to sell two diamonds in Frankfurt.' She carefully feels his head and tries to straighten Ante Allevic's upper body. There's a long piece of iron on the floor next to the chair.

The turn-of-the-century flat has a large sleeper couch and a 'drink niche' bench, in front of it a smoking table, two stools. The lounge chair belongs to the same corner.

### III

'No one on their own is clever enough.' She wants to get some water to clean the blood off his head. She lifts one of Allevic's eyelids with a dish towel (to avoid leaving fingerprints) she's grabbed from the kitchen; observes the white of the Yugoslavian eye. 'She gently blows on it.' She's hoping for a sign of life. She lights a match and holds it before Allevic's mouth. Checks his pulse. She can't feel a thing through the dish towel; a silk scarf she grabs from out of the neighbouring room where Karl Schleich lives doesn't improve matters. She's got to speak with Schleich, her pimp, right away. She runs down Taunusstraße, Moselstraße, Münchner Straße, finds him at 'Studio Luxemburg'.

INGRID: Allevic is lying in the study. Dead.

SCHLEICH: In your study?

INGRID: No, in the front room.

SCHLEICH: Heart attack?

INGRID: Struck on the head. Metal object.

SCHLEICH: You're crazy.

INGRID: Stay calm. You have to let it sink in first.

SCHLEICH: Why are you being so calm?

The two have known each other for eight years. Each of them a professional in their respective fields. They walk back like they always do: Moselstraße, Niddastraße.

Ingrid, ash-blonde hair in summer, somewhat darker in winter or when she doesn't wash it. Born in a large village in Upper Hesse. 'As she promised to have strong bones, he followed her to the room.' 'She wanted to attract attention by means of an unusual figure. One year later, she weighed only 28 kilos.' 'At 23, she threw herself out of a second-storey window of her parents' home during a family gathering. At the time, she was having an affair with an older man. After her fall, she began to lose weight again.' 'She secretly obtained large quantities of laxatives to combat her constipation. Over the course of the year, she developed an addiction to stimulants.' 'To become "uninhibited" she took great amounts of *nocturnettes*.' 'Evenings, she regularly drank a few bottles of beer.' Since finding herself under Karl's influence, she's been eating regularly, has professional ambition. She is professionally successful because of her skills, not her body type. 'My clients produce their pleasure themselves with the help of the expertly triggered fantasies.'

Karl Schleich is on file as a pimp. In reality: burglary specialist.[6] He investigates opportunities for breaking-and-entering (e.g. into a kiosk closed at night via a long, tube-like corridor through the wall into a fur store which, on the firewall side to the kiosk, is not secured). Schleich is responsible for such planning. A specialist in wall-breakthroughs arrives on the evening flight from Milan, he is woken up by Schleich around 3.30 a.m., has breakfast, carries out his job and is driven back to the airport by Schleich to catch the 8.15 a.m. flight to Milan. The furs are kept in a shack in the Taunus woods.

---

6 That the criminal police have never suspected Schleich is partly because he was booked in their files for immoral offences, i.e. a fundamentally different form of activity.

## IV

Bertrand Russel, *Power* (London, 1938), p. 297: '[T]here must be two police forces and two Scotland Yards, one designed, as at present, to prove guilt, the other to prove innocence.'

Schleich held a candle in front of Allevic's mouth to no avail; though it dripped wax onto the dead man's mouth, he didn't want Ingrid's hands to support the man's head because he knew that it was best not to change its position at all in the case of severe head injury. Lying down on the ground across from the slain man and confidently placing an ear to his chest, Schleich still hopes it is not a 'permanent misfortune'. For that would spell his and Ingrid's misfortune. They'd seen the dead before, in pensions, beaten to death by thugs; in their hurry, they had never been able to observe them up close; had they hung around, they would have been dragged into the deaths as witnesses.

'He's alive,' Schleich said, to take the absurdity out of the situation. He made this assumption provisionally. They wrapped the Yugoslavian in blankets. Ingrid brought a hot water bottle out of the kitchen. The blow had deformed the skull, at least that's what it looked like in the artificial light. The shallow wound, flecked with splinters of bone, hair and blood, was dripping. Carefully, as Ingrid would normally have handled a customer's inflamed genitals ('they're not made of rubber'), she placed two terry towels and a silk blouse around the edges of the wound.

They walked over to Westendstraße, where the amateur Schmitz/Mera couple lived. On their way, they passed police patrols, but the latter were only interested in the waning demonstration of squatters on a property on Kettenhofweg. A police squad burst out of Lindenstraße, beating up students running off to the west. Cool evening air. At the end of April, the trees on Bockenheimer Landstraße are already wilted, as in autumn.

## V

The amateur couple sits opposite the angry professionals in the light of a floor lamp. The 'friends'—for two years now they've regularly gone out together—observe each other like 'strange dogs'.

SCHLEICH: You all are crazy.

SCHMITZ: Not in the least. The dead guy's in your apartment, not ours. That's decisive.

SCHLEICH: I told you, there was no way we were going to go along. That means you have to give up your crazy plan.

SCHMITZ: I have no idea what you're talking about. He's in your place.

SCHLEICH: We know you wanted to get the stones.

SCHMITZ: Between the two of us that may be clear. But as far as the police are concerned, he's in your place.

INGRID: Who's talking about the police?

SCHMITZ: Well now, that's reasonable.

SCHLEICH: What does *reasonable* mean here?

SCHMITZ: What's reasonable is leaving the police out of it.

SCHLEICH: They'll show up as soon as you try to unload the stones somewhere. So, out with the stones now.

SCHMITZ: Forget about that. I'd rather turn you all in. Then you'd have to explain how the dead man got into your apartment.

SCHLEICH: You have a set of keys to our apartment.

SCHMITZ: We threw them away.

Schleich walks up to Schmitz, punches him in the face. Heike Mera screams, tries to attack Schleich. Ingrid helps him. Schmitz escapes into the hallway, turns the key, calls through the door:

SCHMITZ: I'm going to the police.

INGRID: And how do you know anything about the murder?

SCHMITZ: I'm going to report the Yugoslavian as missing.

Schmitz doesn't take off, although he could reach the street from the hallway. Schleich and Ingrid are holding Schmitz's beloved hostage. But they are worried that, in an emergency, Schmitz will abandon her. There's no way to break open the door without making noise. They go through the living room. Heike Mera—whose arms Ingrid, with Schleich's help, is twisting—doesn't know where the diamonds are.

## VI

'The poisonous little man in his father's shoes.'

'A daughter from a very good family.'

Dietrich Schmitz and Heike Mera attempt to establish an ordered existence: to be 'good'. For Schmitz, this means: walking around in patent-leather shoes, a light-green tracksuit, *just like* his father, a criminal investigator, carefully dressed according to his official position, at the same time *absolutely* deviant. A brooch on Schmitz's tie the colour of pomade. The boundlessness of Schmitz's ambition determines the means. The fact that he doesn't plan things all the way through leads the professional Schleich to regard him with contempt. For two years Schmitz has been planning, together with the professional Gerschwind, a break-in to steal furs. He does not execute the plan. Mera, lacking in influence, urges him to get on the 'right path', but wants to emigrate to Brazil with him too; this is why the amateur couple needs cash. Now Schleich is amazed to realize that these amateurs are 'doing' something after all.

That same night, Ingrid and Schleich find the diamonds in a boathouse in Bad Vilbel where Schmitz had kept a collapsible boat.

## VII

At 3 in the morning, Schleich and Ingrid return to their Yugoslavian. 'He won't get any better lying down.' Schleich thinks the dead man is still breathing, if faintly.

It is Saturday/Sunday. They wrap Allevic in a carpet and carry him to a small van which Schleich has borrowed. They have to wait until 6. The two doze in each other's arms for a few hours. Then they drive to a structure in the Taunus woods, lay Allevic down on a wooden palette.

Ingrid is waiting outside the office of the abortionist Dennerlein, wants to persuade him to have a look at the half-dead man. Dennerlein: The case is too dangerous for me.

The reality: he does not feel up to treating the headwound she's described. Ingrid has to get Schleich involved, whose threats Dennerlein is forced to take seriously. He is now going with them. He feels Allevic's head, consults a handbook on head surgery. At the moment, his knowledge is not enough. Schleich can see as much. For Dennerlein, it is essential that the two don't take him to be a quitter. He travels to Mainz, asks an assistant doctor he knows at the university clinic.

Dennerlein takes care of the headwound. They crush the pills they pour into the half-dead man. It turns out Allevic can swallow. Ingrid speaks to him. Later, she said she had kept the damaged brain active during the critical phase so that it did not die completely. She benefits from the fact that she is now well rested. She has learnt how to talk to customers like a teller of fairy tales.

## VIII

Ingrid knows Pfuller, they call him the father of whores, a criminal investigator, he is susceptible to cash benefits and the occasional, rather specialized sex act. She asks him for help.

Pfuller steps into the Schmitz/Heike Mera flat.

PFULLER (*points to his badge*): Criminal police.

SCHMITZ (*cocky*): And you want . . . ?

PFULLER: You former police yourself?

SCHMITZ: What's that got to do with anything?

PFULLER: I just have a few questions.

SCHMITZ: I don't answer any questions. What's the charge?

PFULLER (*forces his way in*): Let's see if you don't answer my questions.

SCHMITZ: What is it?

PFULLER: I'm not going to tell *you* until you tell *me* a thing or two.

SCHMITZ: I have nothing to say.

PFULLER: That's interesting indeed. You don't have anything to say to me?

SCHMITZ: What is it then? You can't deal with me this way.

PFULLER: Let's wait and see how I deal with you. First, I've got to follow up a lead.

SCHMITZ: Then why don't you take me with you to the station?

PFULLER: How do you know I won't?

SCHMITZ: Because you're sitting here. If you wanted to arrest me, you'd have brought along a colleague.

PFULLER: False conclusion. Maybe I've got reasons to show up here alone?

This lasts an hour. Schmitz and Mera, who cannot interpret the purpose of this visit, take the 4.45 train to Barcelona.

## IX

Dennerlein: 'The client can now be transported.' For brief moments Ante Allevic is conscious. He is breathing, sleeps a lot. Ingrid 'talks' with him every day for four to five hours, without paying attention to the meaning of the words.

They wrap him in blankets, place him in a large suitcase with sizeable air holes drilled in the bottom; they place the suitcase on bricks, so that there is a space between it and the floor of the van. They pile camouflage material on top.

That night, they take the autobahn towards Karlsruhe. They cross the border to Austria on forest roads. Allevic groans a few times. Once over the Yugoslavian border, they stop in a wooded area. Ingrid talks to the now-awake Allevic for an hour: little reaction.

In Ljubljana, Ingrid and Schleich drop Allevic off with the porter of a district hospital. Allevic's pockets are later found to contain identity papers and two precious stones.

## X

Schleich and Ingrid Fahle, who took turns driving through the night, are back at home. The exhausting labour of the past three weeks: unpaid. But their cooperation creates trust. They celebrate with a pleasant hour at a cost of 50 marks. Ingrid says: 'Maybe giving Allevic just the two diamonds to cover his expenses was the wrong thing to do, maybe we should have given him cash.' With greater experience, her technique will become more perfect.

Film stills from *Die Macht der Gefühle* (The Power of Emotion), final sequence: Undoing of a crime through mutual cooperation, 1983.

## A SATURDAY IN OCTOBER 1929

The BASIC IDEA was not what Dr Erwin Zacke would later claim to his wife: that they should enjoy a comfortable life for a few more years before having children, but SUSPICION, CAUTION. The way they were sitting together, no basic idea could arise. After morning drinks, they just sat around until midday (it was a Saturday), then continued to sit together until evening drinks, waiting for a snack the maids were preparing in the kitchen.

- It would be a sin not to do it. In a quarter of an hour, we're done (Zacke said). Everything's here. Karl (Erwin's friend, surgical colleague) does it the short way.
- Is it painful?

The young woman would have liked to keep her child but didn't want to make things difficult. It was a matter of illusion. She could imagine being a young mother and she could also imagine being 'free of parental duties', 'we can go travelling'. And though they were sitting around the table, dressed, she was uneasy about being touched in an intimate place by the guest who, as the more experienced doctor, was to perform the operation. She was undecided.

- Not everyone can have something like this done on the weekend and in their own house to boot. This is luxury (the husband said).

He was overdoing it, for seizing the opportunity was not his motive.

He had married the young woman just about two months previously within a week of having met. But he was unsure whether she was 'untouched', hadn't checked at the right time. He didn't want to appear 'medical' at that moment either. So it now seemed more 'prudent' for him to get rid of the child, if with regret in the case it had indeed been conceived by him.

- Let us sit here in peace for a while (the young woman said).
- Karl can do everything in a quarter of an hour (Erwin answered).
- Not against her will (a guest opined).
- I've got to think (said she).

She wanted to win some time.

Those at table together were fairly drunk. This condition benefited the defence of the womb because it made those involved sluggish.

- It is now 5.45 p.m. (the zealous one warned). If we want to be finished by 6.30, we've got to get going.
- Don't be pushy.
- If we're done by 7, we can slice the ham and set out a cold duck. The Liesenbergs are coming at 9, and at 11 there will be hot sausages.
- Now that's what I call a *programme* (Karl, the head surgeon, said).
- Let me think about it (the young woman resisted).

If she's this interested in the child, Erwin thought, maybe it's because she'll see a former lover in it. There was much about his rapid success that confused the man. He pressed hard:

- Well, come on.
- Do let me sit here a moment longer (the young woman resisted).

The doctor and his friend went up to surgery and prepared the operation.

The young woman, staring at a row of lights downstairs, felt alone after a while, went upstairs and let the men do what they so urgently wanted. When they returned from their activities, the maids were clattering in the hatchway to the dining room. They had put on their bonnets. Evening fell. This could be seen through the greenhouse windows. Now certainty had been established.

## THE MAN WITHOUT QUALITIES

A German auteur filmmaker had prepared a proposal but had been unable to submit it to the committees. This was supposed to be his next attempt. He was interested in filming Robert Musil's *The Man without Qualities*, which some consider to be THE NOVEL OF THE CENTURY.

The producer asked the director:

- Do you mean to direct yourself?
- Yes.
- Could you give me an outline, I'm unfamiliar with the novel, or rather I haven't read it all the way through.
- How far did you get?
- The beginning.
- Like most people.
- If you can summarize the content in a few sentences?
- The man without qualities . . .
- That's clear. He's got no qualities. But why not?
- That's the title.

- Isn't that what the book's about?
- It has to do with a pair of siblings.
- With or without incest?
- It's not entirely clear. Some passages towards the end point more towards incest, others speak against it. The man's named Ulrich, his sister Agathe.
- Aha. And the content?
- You mean the plot?
- What happens?
- The man has no qualities. That says something about the twentieth century. The book contains an astute analysis of the twentieth century.
- And what comes out of it?
- That's not in the book.
- Maybe you have to add it in the film?
- I wanted to stick with what's in the book.
- Yes, but you would have to tell the viewer the plot. You can't say this Ulrich had no qualities, and that there's no plot either, and as for the century, we don't know what's going to come out of it, and the movie has no beginning, no end and certainly no middle. That would be unsuitable for a preview, for example.
- Talking like you do, you could talk any material into submission.
- *The Man without Qualities* is quite a good title in and of itself. Makes you think.
- So you agree with the material?

- Let's put it this way: I was impressed by your point that you can talk up any material with the right expressions. Lots of condensed versions, and then we say that these are famous pieces. At that point, the viewer has to pay attention.
- Just summaries?
- Yes. And a lot of them. The FILM WITHOUT QUALITIES, so to speak. A young woman who can't decide on anything doesn't get the man she thinks she wants either. She doesn't want the other guy. The years pass. Her child is killed in an accident, and no one knows if she will ever see her husband again. The one she simply *thought* she loved has, in the meantime, died. 'Gone with the wind!' Great stuff!
- You could include that straight off.
- Say, that makes for a wonderful guessing game!
- But what I had in mind was a film about THE MAN WITHOUT QUALITIES . . .
- I'm really quite impressed with my solution, I must say. We've got to leave the *qualities* bit out. *The Man*, that would be quite a title, would also have something to do with the twentieth century.
- But I'd decided . . .
- Yeah, I know, but I don't consider your solution effective. Don't ask me if you don't want to accept my suggestion.
- What kind of suggestion?
- You're not listening.

# THEY DID NOT COME TO ANY CONCLUSION

## A FILM PRODUCER'S MISUNDERSTANDINGS

'Vast amounts of discriminative ability'

*Niklas Luhmann*

Today we introduce you to a madman who wants to introduce a new type of film to television. He doesn't want films to have plots but simply to describe differences. He'll explain that to you in a moment, said the assistant to the producer. And it was at that moment that Markus M., a commercial artist who had decided to become a film director, walked through the door.

- And what is your film about?
- It's not about anything, it shows differences, or a difference, so to speak. Cold/warm, bright/dark, velvety-soft/rough-as-concrete, but also light dark-blonde/pale brunette, it's got to do with nuances, I tell the hairdresser: just on the edge of dark-blonde, and then I add: light brunette, that's important.
- But surely you have a storyline, right?
- Nope, don't need one. Take your fingertip, for example, it's different from mine.
- And you think that viewers want to see a fingertip? What do you call this new genre of yours?
- We've still got to come up with a name!
- I see. And financing? What differences did you have in mind for the beginning?
- That's something we'd have to think about. You shouldn't approach filming with any preconceptions.
- What kind of budget were you thinking about?

- Between 3 and 6 million dollars.
- Couldn't you make the project into a low-budget production?
- Then it would cost 160,000 marks.
- And if it's a real film?
- Then it would be a bit cheaper.
- Interesting. And you can film differences?
- That's what I said.
- That's interesting. Commercial?
- You mean commercial differences?
- Can one employ the films commercially?
- As a producer you should know.
- I do. I'm just asking.
- On a practical level, what does a film producer actually do . . . ?
- That's a wide field.
- As opposed to what?

They did not come to any conclusion.

# WANDERERS BY NIGHT

'That I can see, that I can hear, are things I do not deserve; but my feelings, those I truly deserve, these herons over white beaches, these wanderers by night, the hungry vagabonds that take my heart as their highroad . . .'

Ingeborg Bachmann, The Thirtieth Year<br>(translated by Michael Bullock)

FIGURE 3. Summer seminar at Harvard University, 1955. *Far left* (x): Henry Kissinger, seminar director; *fourth from left* (x) Ingeborg Bachmann.

## EXECUTING AN ELEPHANT

I, who venerate every quarter I make, from Odessa originally and in New York for the last two years, have the honour or serving the great Edwin S. Porter as a research assistant and grip electric. Engineer Porter is a director employed by the Edison Manufacturing Company. As one of the advance troops, I've been on set since 4 in the morning. The entertainment venues of Coney Island, where we're filming, are asleep. The sun is expected to come from the direction of the sea.

The beast, which looked like other elephants, had no malice in its round eyes, it just stood in its tent, straw beneath its feet, 'waiting to be executed'. The keepers, I assumed, didn't like the animal as it had killed three of their colleagues. They looked after it as per the dictates of their schedule. The animal crushed turnips and hay in its mouth. Gazing trustingly into the morning, it had probably forgotten its misdeeds or didn't even recognize them as such.

Two hours later, the camera is carried in. The keepers led the delinquent animal to an open forecourt where ropes put a distance between it and the spectators. Electric cables have been attached to its left front and right hind foot. Elephants are quadrupeds; it is sufficient to paralyse one limb on each side to immobilize both.

'Ready!' Porter called out. He had designed the camera, which is also a patented film-projection device. The crew did not possess the refinement of 1904, which marked the climax of Edison Studios. That's why there weren't any light sources positioned at the elephant's back, which would have defined the shaking animal's shape against the horizon.[7] Be that as it may, the elephant didn't tremble—it just stood there quietly. Viewers were prompted to buy tickets. The

---

7 Without such 'highlights', the grey skin does not stand out from the horizon. The camera was angled 'inland'.

crew waited for more people to arrive on the suburban trains to watch 'electrocution in Coney Island's electric chair'.

Around 11, the keepers turned on the electrodes. The giant reared. I had the impression I could see its muscles tense. Smoke by the shackled 'elephant feet'. Then the giant body of protein collapsed onto its left side, a heap of suffering.

The guards and film operators were horrified, seemed agitated. Porter said: 'This will be a sensation.' The film cans holding the negatives are marked with the company name, the date. 'Title: *Electrocuting an Elephant*'. The keepers, used to feeding the animal, hosing it down and disposing of its faeces, irritated by the death of their three colleagues, even though they had taken their places, had disappeared. They had not said anything in the way of critique.

I didn't say anything either. The 35 mm recordings of the death penalty on the African elephant ensured an unusual number of spectators. The following year, countless cinemagoers watched the few minutes of the film, presumably seeing the images as proof that they themselves were still alive.

In the meantime, I have watched the film 14 times. I can say: you see very little. After about one and a quarter minutes, you can make out a cloud of smoke in the grey, the moment the animal's feet began to burn. Followed by the spectacular collapse. The scene does not remind me of an 'electrocution in the electric chair'. The impact of the strip has everything to do with its title, the advance notice. Later, we shot the film *The Execution of President McKinley's Murderer* (and surpassed the audience size of the elephant picture). The recording was staged, the gassed man an extra.

In my opinion, the most incredible moment, however, wasn't filmed: the elephant allowing itself to be led calmly onto the forecourt, he who could have broken free and trampled any obstacle underfoot.

## THE EMPEROR OF MY TRUST

The Roman emperor Julianus, whom the Christians later called Apostata ('the apostate'), was the last ruler to trust in the pagan gods. In his decrees, he stipulated that Christian communities pay compensation for any damages they caused, for the destruction of any consecrated temple.[8]

The emperor, with his pointed beard the beloved of the legionaries, led the Roman army against the king of the Parthians. The latter persuaded two Parthian nobles to have their noses mutilated and appear before the emperor as alleged defectors. A march into the flank of the Parthian army would be promising. The emperor believed the mutilated men. After 30 kilometres of marching in the Namib desert, he noticed the trap. The Parthian cavalry quickly attacked. The emperor did not have time to put on his armour. A spear hit his liver. The soldiers managed to catch him as he fell from his horse and bring him to a tent. In the meantime, the Parthians had decided the battle. The pagan emperor questioned that small group of loyal soldiers gathered around him, which included numerous famous doctors of antiquity. Did he stand a chance? None. The friends did not lie to one another. In the terrifying hour after midnight, the wound burst open, the emperor died.

This was the bishops' impertinent revenge, they who felt aggrieved by the emperor's decrees. The spear that pierced the emperor came from Christian hand.

---

8 It is to this emperor that the world owes the principle: 'When in doubt, favour the accused.' Even when he ruled as governor and emperor in Gaul, he exercised his right of veto in criminal proceedings. The prosecutor Delfidius questioned the emperor in public: 'How should one convict and punish a defendant who denies his offence?' Julianus replied: 'Certainly not by taking the accusation as proof of guilt.'

## STAR WARS

'Only a nasty dog can mock Russia's life in a nasty way.'

*Aleksandr A. Blok*

At that moment I was proud of our president, Valentin Falin said. He allowed the other vehicles to go on ahead. Our delegation was on its way to the airport. The summit was unsuccessful, had been broken off. Something which had never happened before.

The atmosphere over Reykjavik was pervaded by lows, an oppressive, cold, changeable weather formation that does not suit us Russians. The meeting took place in a villa on a peninsula that stretched far out into the bay. There we sat, opposite one another. Our assistants in the adjoining rooms provided the documents for the trial.

We were prepared, Falin said. We were of the impression that the other side was unprepared, disconcerted by the electoral campaign, wasn't up to the level of what was being negotiated. We were offering—and I differed from the president in this—emphatic disarmament on land, at sea and in the air, including liquidation of the intercontinental weapons that constituted our strength.

The US delegation welcomed this proposal but wanted to maintain the R&D aspect of their Strategic Defence Initiative (SDI) concerning an anti-ballistic missile programme designed to shoot down nuclear missiles in space.

We discussed it back in our rooms. Our brains as if stupefied by the weather, but, with a lot of tea, stimulated nevertheless. We're looking at the problem incorrectly, the general secretary said, when we only consider the technology. 'Star Wars' is for the birds. The catapults we're constructing out of dirt, sand and metal can respond to the technological finesse of these satellites that are capable of carrying laser weapons and are orbiting the globe at an altitude of 10,000 kilometres with ROBUSTNESS. But there's another side to 'Star Wars', one for which we have no compensation: the MILITARY-INDUSTRIAL COMPLEX in the US is using the SDI project to engineer a tunnel that leads directly into US budget plans. THIS TECHNOLOGY, not the technical ability to operate in space, is the danger. Budgets march separately, but strike together.

That was the moment, Falin said, the president won me over.[9] Today my relationship with Gorbachev has soured. We could have developed a lovely relationship from what transpired in Reykjavik. I still regret not having intervened when Gorbachev, as General Secretary of the Central Committee, was arrested. I came too late. But even though I was late, I could have persuaded the party to intervene.

## CLEAR MOSCOW EVENINGS, WHEN THE NORTHWEST WIND BLOWS

During the brief period at the turn of the year 1923/24 when it was uncertain whether the working class or Stalin's bureaucracy would take over the party, Dr Kleve, a private scholar, who was a regular at a health resort in the Harz mountains and enjoyed the beneficial physical effects of the Life Reform movement[10] (it now breathed within him), took the train to the capital of the revolution: Moscow. Recommended as a good tip to the organizational leaders of an

---

9 He ended the conference, did not accept any excuses from the opposing side. In so doing, he forced the other superpower to give up their plans for WAR IN SPACE.

10 The same Jungborn Naturopathic Institute in the Harz that Franz Kafka had visited.

international socialist circle, he was to give a lecture. He was received at the Belorussian railway station, given noble lodgings, equipped with food coupons. One of the scurrying women who kept the grand hotel brought the newcomer a bowl of cherries. After that, Kleve was forgotten. The presentation was cancelled for organizational reasons; no new date was given. And so Dr Kleve settled into his room, 'making use of the time' as if sitting in a room at the foot of the Harz mountains. As long as he had pencils and paper and access to a selection of food that did not require him to eat pork, his behaviour was the same.

Dr Kleve had a theory that was objectively suitable for solving the problems of the Soviet Union in 1924. And in the sense of labour opposition.[11] But Kleve did not speak Russian, and German-speaking comrades in those days were always in a hurry. He found no one to whom he could have explained the elaborate core of his theory. Hence, he had a problem: 'In the opinion of the Socialist congresses, a theory becomes reality when it grips the masses.' In other words, if a theory is correct, the masses will take it up. The fact that they 'take it up', that they come to it of their own accord, verifies the theory. But no masses made their way to Dr Kleve's hotel room.[12]

---

[11] At the centre of Kleve's theory was a combination of Alexander Bogdanov's *Proletkult*, Abilev's *Political Economy of Labour Power* and selected rules from Welliglott's project, *Lebensquell*, to which the mountain institute in the Harz was also oriented. Thus equipped, in three years, the labour opposition would be unbeatable.

[12] Perhaps Leningrad would have been a place for Kleve where he would have had more luck. A detail of his theory was that under socialism the concept of nation's capital had to be modified. The capital is not in any central place (since, after all, the patriots carry it around in their hearts and all central points are in the labour process, that is, in the machinery itself). But since the TRUE SOCIAL RELATIONSHIP needs a corresponding place that can be

Were the theories of the 'magician' all alone in the grand hotel waiting for someone to question him thus disproved? Why doesn't a poor system—which, stockpiling failure, doesn't require any quick success—ask the only one in the city that knows the answers? A 37° MESSAGE IN A BOTTLE, straight from the Harz?

After six weeks of patiently adapting to NOTHING HAPPENING, Dr Kleve took the train across the two borders back to Germany.

### GALINA STAROVOITOVA

Even the experienced body menders of the Pathological Institute of the University of St Petersburg were unable to make the bullet-riddled body 'attractive'. They wrapped the remains in a sack-like container and placed the head on top, the restored pale face. The ghastly head wound disappeared under a hood like that of a monk. Thus prepared, the prominent politician was transported and laid out at the Russian Museum of Ethnography. Celebrities from all corners of the country attended her farewell ceremony.

- Her parents?
- Father was an engineer. Defence industry. In 1940, moved from Leningrad to Chelyabinsk. Built the T-34. Later in Baikonur. Worked on the lunar rover. Stage management.
- Her mother?

---

grasped by the senses, the METROPOLE OF THE WORKERS is in Leningrad, with an enclave for the south in Odessa, for the centre in Omsk, for the East in Vladivostok, for the orthodox in Moscow and for the lonely North in Arkhangelsk. All these components are the equivalent of 'capital city'.

- Defence. Got to know each other via a friend at a Christmas party. Her first child: Galina. The one at their heads there is the father. Outlived her.

The two journalists from a private Moscow TV station exchanging this information spoke in a whisper. Via their monitors they could see what the three cameras set up near the sarcophagus were capturing. They didn't realize that their booth was 'on air', so that the viewers of the TV station received more extensive information than they were used to.

- Grandparents?
- Paternal grandfather a tractor driver. Activist from 1917. Married to the daughter of a Cossack from the south. Maternal grandparents: artisans, activists of electrification of 1921. Galina has a 26-year-old son. He has two children. You can see them there (points to the detail of a photograph on Camera 2).
- So, all in all, five generations.
- Yes. And shot like that. It's hard to believe!
- Five years' worth of material for our paper. The same goes for your station.

Galina Starovoitova, Duma deputy, lively, surrounded by colleagues, was seen on the Friday evening Moscow–St Petersburg flight. Together with her press secretary Linkov, she had already arranged further appointments. It was most likely a contract killing.[13] Her killers were waiting for her in the stairwell of her apartment building.

---

13 Twenty shots from a machine gun; she tumbled down the iron stairs. Her press secretary, Linkov, seriously wounded, managed to alert the police with his mobile phone. The head of domestic security, who flew in to the scene of the crime that very night: Why wasn't the execution carried out more professionally?

FIGURE 4. Milky Way.

# 20 BILLION YEARS BEFORE CHRIST

## FROM THE AEONS CHRONICLE
## OF THE MONK ANDREI BITOV

**20 billion years BCE**
A primordial ocean charged with energy in which matter and antimatter coexist.

**11 billion years BCE**
Drastic cooling off. Transition from an untransparent to a transparent universe.

**14 billion years BCE – 4.9 billion years BCE**
Cosmic process in which the solar system is formed.

**4 billion years BCE**
In Guyana, the oldest rock forms, composed of iron silicate and magnesium.

**3.8 billion years BCE**
The temperature of the earth's surface sinks below the boiling point of water. Like the Biblical flood to come, the water masses condense and form the first ocean. It covers almost the entire surface of the earth. 'Inanimate life.'

**3.3 billion years BCE**
The moon's orbit stabilizes.

**3 billion years BCE**[14]
Formation of a single continent surrounded by a vast ocean. Oldest diamonds. Cocci in the oceans form spherical clusters, acaryotes.

---

14 Chronicler Andrei Bitov, for his part, is against the designation BCE for the earliest dates of this chronicle. In his view, none of the events that establish the cosmos and the earth so early relate to this date.

**1 billion years BCE**
A flood of solar winds bombard the upper atmosphere, creating the ozone layer. This shadow replaces the protection that the water layers of the ocean had previously provided for life. Amphibian attempts.

**800 million years BCE**
Large active volcanoes on Mars, including Olympus.

**680 million years BCE**
First jellyfish.

**550 million years BCE**
The earth spins quickly. In the Cambrian period, a day lasts 21 hours, a year 420 days.

**380 million years BCE**
Leafy plants. Arachnids = dry-land spiders. The Comoros-island coelacanths.

**300 million years BCE**
Pangaea. The first forests.[15]

**245 million years BCE**
'Eoraptor', 7 cm-large saurian reptile. First planetary natural disaster. 98 per cent of species eliminated.

**200 million years BCE**
Tethys Ocean. Palms grow in Greenland, conifers in Alaska. Dinosaurs. The body-size of our ancestors between 5 and 20 cm.

**90 million years BCE**
Madagascar separates from East Africa, joins with India. Drifts towards the northeast. Cretaceous snakes.

---

15  Possessed today by Arab sheikhs.

**55 million years BCE**
India breaks away from Madagascar and joins Eurasia. The Indian continental floe moves 3,000 kilometres northwards.

**15 million years BCE**
The Antarctic separates from South Africa. 'The earth's refrigerator'.

**12 million years BCE**
'Oreopithecus bamboli', an ancestor, lives in Tuscany.

Working on this chronicle, the monk Bitov writes, I am forced to counteract a mistake that many of my colleagues believe. In a chronicle staggered over time, 'past times' seem to disappear into the 'present'. The new times, however, do not even causally follow the old; rather, they are INTERCONNECTED. How do I know this? From the oldest texts. The primordial ocean mentioned above has existed for 20 billion years. What does it do? If you can speak of *doing* with such a giant creature, that is? Wherever our universe touches this ocean, matter is created. New at every moment. If the universe, the starry worlds we see, were to detach themselves for a moment from these 'waters', the primordial ocean, we would be nothing, as we are created anew every moment. This, according to the church father Diodorus, gives us chroniclers permission to deviate from the erroneous time data given in the Old Testament, for the resurrection is not in the future but at any given moment (and not in the form of the Lord Jesus Christ), it recreates the aeons and what we consider to be matter. Matter is always there for a moment and not there for a moment.

Our Greek Orthodox church, Andrei Bitov continues, does not practise exclusion. It got lost on its way from Byzantium to Russia. Otherwise, I, a pagan in monk's robes, would no longer be in office. I am by no means prepared to attribute the marvellous paradoxes that my chronicle shows, its dowry (Diodorus says: 'Like goods washed up on the coastlines of our knowledge that tell of failed ships'), to the WILFULNESS OF A SINGLE INDIVIDUAL. I would feel embarrassed in front of all my online contacts.

There are, however, miracles enough hidden within the text of nature. I only mention the fact that the universe (and now I don't just mean our barge, but all universes that emerge from the primordial ocean) foresaw conditions at the time of zero that only developed after 10 billion years. How could it have foreseen the SUITABLE so early if it was not interconnected throughout time, from beginning to end? Allow me to mention the energy levels of carbon, beryllium and helium. Because they fit one on top of another, we chroniclers are alive. I have counted 40 phylogenetically different kinds of insects whose ancestors across the globe could never have been in contact with one another but who have the same regulator gene for the structure of the eye. Remote control? Through whom if not the animals themselves? I call this, Bitov writes, the power of recall within the chronicle. It makes 'all times new'.[16]

**2.4 million years BCE**
End of post-volcanic winter. The oldest human known to us. Small in stature, between 1.20 and 1.60 metres tall, brain volume 700 ml, with straight thigh bones.

---

[16] We modern monks trust the forces of self-regulation. Let me remind you of Fermi's experiment. In Chicago, he created a pair of photons. He separates the twins, fixes them in separate containers, one of which is taken by plane to Tokyo as quickly as possible, the other kept in Chicago. Fermi then changed the condition of the latter. His colleague in Tokyo reported by telegraph the exact same change in the Tokyo twin. This could not have been achieved by one of God's fingers. We believe in self-regulation.

**700,000 years BCE**

'Homo loquens' or 'Atlanthropus' in Algeria. Probably the first human to speak a roughly articulated language. Ten consonants and three vowel-like sounds.

**100,000 years BCE**

Discovery of the earth's orbit around the sun. Slight greenhouse effect. Dwarf elephants go extinct.

**8,000 years BCE**

'The Sahara becomes a swamp.'

**7,683 years BCE**

The oldest tree whose annual rings have been measured. Later, an even older tree is discovered: Tasmania, 10,500 BCE. Hidden in stones at a depth of 2,000 metres are fungi that are 20,000 years old. Bacteria found in rock salt in Silesia are 200,000 years old (discovered by Knappig).

**3,000 years BCE**

On being and having. Papyrus paper out of the dirty pith of the papyrus plant. The pith is cut into strips, soaked in water, worked into a pasty mass, stacked crosswise and formed into a writing surface by hammering.

**2,000/1,400 years BCE**

14 language groups: Aryo-Indian, Iranian, Anatolian, Thocarian, Armenian, Gallic, Italian, Celtic, Germanic, Slovakian, Baltic, Albanian, Thracian-Phrygian, Veneto-Illyrian. Minoan-Cretan hieroglyphs: Linear B script.[17]

---

17 At present, the diversity of the world, Bitov writes, expresses itself in 6,000 languages. In Asia 2,034, in Africa 1,995, in the Pacific region 1,341, in America 949, in Europe 209. The extravagance of the Caucasian languages is attributed to Asia. Half of all languages have fewer than 10,000 speakers, of

**753 BCE**

The founding of Rome. Legend.

**643 BCE**

Polished optical lenses in Asia Minor.

**531 BCE**

Development of the first machines. Adyta v. Taranto, Philon v. Byzantium.

**1 CE**

Gaul has 25 million inhabitants.

**3 CE**

First history of the world in 14 volumes.[18]

---

which 2/3 have fewer than a thousand. A rescue expedition is needed to secure the hidden messages about humanity's past from these language genres threatened with extinction. On the Internet, English is dominant, at 57.4 per cent frequency, Xaver Holtzmann, who is often in conversation with Bitov online, adds. Chinese, with a frequency of just 4.4 per cent, is the more useful system for computers. Portuguese, Dutch and French with 4.2 to 1.5 per cent are not dominant. Mandarin is spoken more frequently with 885 million speakers compared to English with its 470 million (including those who use it as a second language) and 332 million Spanish speakers. For the actual language of Europe in the year 1,000 (192,000 speakers), Holtzmann counts 10,800 Latin students and participants worldwide on the Internet.

18  Still in relation to the third century, Bitov therefore quotes a Hellenistic author, a pagan with far-reaching knowledge. The church, Bitov writes, is an offspring of the cosmos, and it only has a chance after the advent of papyrus (3,000 BCE), and initially as a pagan church. It is too young to observe the RIGHT OF SELF-DETERMINATION OF TIME, which precedes the right of peoples to self-determination.

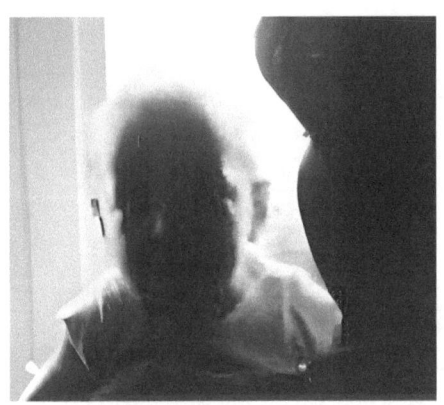

FIGURE 5. 'Trustworthy'.

Fig. 72. Head of Semnopithecus rubicundus. This and the following figures (from Prof. Gervais) are given to show the odd arrangement and development of the hair on the head.

FIGURE 6. An ancestor. It can do a lot:
(1) catch prey; (2) seek out shady hideaways; (3) raise its young in a reasonably relaxed manner; (4) bring them to safety, bring itself to safety; (5) fight for pecking order; bite the offspring of defeated males to death; (6) carefully study to ensure there are no enemies in the vicinity (that there are enough signs that the sounds, smells, colours, vibrations are more or less the same as most nights); (7) FALL ASLEEP. This ancestor falls asleep because it knows it will surely wake up.

What it doesn't like at all: (1) exercising consistent care; (2) being productive; (3) killing things inside itself; (4) killing itself to begin with.

Illustration from Prof. Gervais. 'Odd arrangement of the hair, much hope.'

## MORE ANIMALS ON EARTH THAN STARS IN THE MILKY WAY

### FROM HOLTZMANN'S OPENING BALANCE OF THE 21ST CENTURY

Xaver Holtzmann has had a short burst of speed. Thanks to support from the UNEP (United Nations Environment Programme), the IUCN (International Union for Conservation of Nature) and the WCMC (World Conservation Monitoring Centre).

In a publication, he calculated the number of animals on our planet and compared it with the number of stars in our galaxy. This is significant in the event of a class-action lawsuit should the planet be destroyed.

The stars of the Milky Way, counted with an error rate of 0.3 per cent: 200 billion. The number of animals on earth: 1 trillion. Of those, 10 billion are ants, 300 billion birds.[19]

There are 10,000 people for every elephant, 20,000 for a white stork, 100,000 for a lion, 1,000,000 for a tiger, 5,000,000 for a giant panda and 6 billion for the rarest animal in the wild (there is only one specimen of this parrot species left), the Spix's macaw.

Of interest for class-action suits are pets. 106 million cats (not counting strays), 94 million dogs (not counting strays). And then farm animals: 3 trillion bees, 20 billion other types of animals: 13 billion chickens, 1.3 billion cows, 1 billion sheep, 935 million pigs, 699 million goats, 209 million geese, 246.4 million turkeys, 162.3 million domestic buffalo, 60.9 million horses, 19 million camels, 2.6 million farmed crocodiles.

---

[19] Average value. Estimates range between 200 and 400 billion. This means that there are 50 birds per person and 167 million animals in total.

Added to this is the loss of the planet: oil, coal, mineral resources, enclosed space, antiques.[20] As for birds, Holtzmann lists in detail: city pigeons (rock doves, wild domestic pigeons) 32 million (increasing), red-billed quelea 1.5 billion, skylarks 320 million, barn swallows 15 million, herring gulls 2.3 million, polar bears 1.3 million (stable), yellow-legged flamingos 50,000, European cranes 250,000, Stellar's sea eagles 7,500, red-spotted cockatoos 3,000 (decreasing), Humboldt penguins 20,000, emperor penguins 350,000 (stable).

There are 500 trees for every person, Holtzmann calculates, 6833 m3 of renewable fresh water.

Life on earth weighs 1,850 billion tons. Of those 99 per cent is of a vegetable nature. The biomass of humans amounts to 0.1 billion tons. Every year, 41.5 billion tons are added to the open oceans, 117.5 billion tons on our continents. In the city of Brussels, the inhabitants weigh 7.16 per cent of the city's live weight (i.e. the weight of the city after deducting non-living stones, metals and other urban matter), the rainworms 0.97 per cent, the dogs 0.12 per cent, other animals 0.61 per cent, evil weighs 61 per cent, good 26 per cent, the rest is depletion.

Holtzmann's aim in collecting all this data was to come up with an opening balance of the twenty-first century. The thorough Holtzmann added a balance sheet for 31 December 1799 and 31 December of the year 1000 based on estimates. The data for the year 1000 is imprecise as the date of 31 December can only be determined approximately due to the calendar changes that have taken place in the meantime.

---

20 The loss of profit, i.e. the mineral resources that have not yet been extracted and are still 'ownerless property', is irrelevant for the class action.

FIGURE 7. Weight of Mount Everest: 300 trillion tonnes.

FIGURE 8. The weight of the water mass of the Lago Maggiore: 37 trillion tonnes.

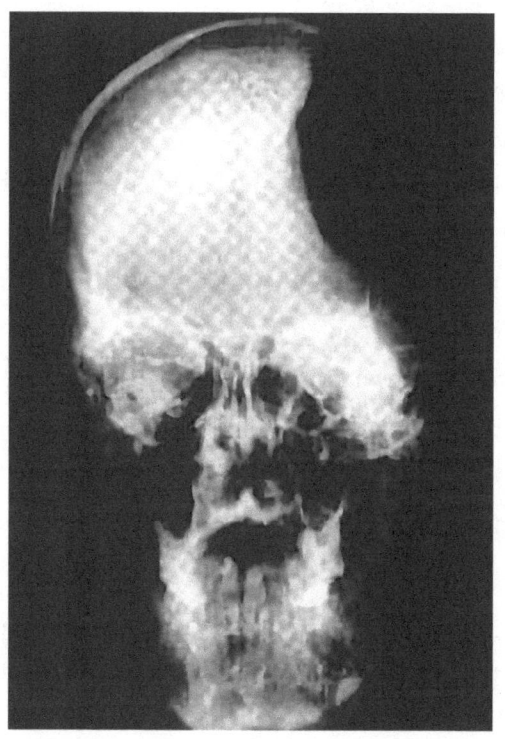

FIGURE 9. Although the patient lost the left hemisphere of his brain in the Vietnam War, he can recognize and compare Arabic numerals. *Exact equations*, however, are difficult.

## THE CONFIDENCE OF CAGED COWS

At the end of his proverbial tether, Gert Hunziger managed to save himself over the Easter break by checking in to a castle hotel. The following exchange took place at one of its group tables.

- What is your profession?
- It corresponds to a ministerial counsellor.
- As you said 'it corresponds to', does that mean you work abroad?
- For the Food and Agriculture Organization—the FAO.
- Ah ha!
- I am coming from the conference in Munich.
- What kind of conference?
- One dealing with food and agriculture.
- Is it still going on?
- It will continue after Easter.
- And now you're here.
- Now I am here.

The man, still nervous from the conference, responded with a smile, e.g. politely, to his neighbour at the table, a young woman who was out of the question for him as an acquaintance during these Easter days. The castle hotel had been recommended because it was known to being amendable for short-term relations. The young woman, busily asking questions, seemed to be radiating too great an earnestness, WILLINGNESS and EARNESTNESS. He could see that from some of the signs: the position of the corners of her mouth, her eyebrows too close together, the position of her neck, her back. She was not to be won over for any easy three-day relationship.

But he was on the run from the past, an exhausted man towards the recent present. On days like that, the future can only be established slowly.

Right before the conference, he'd saved a project in Saudi Arabia at the last minute. He had flown there, organized dry fodder (hay) from Ethiopia and had it flown to Wadi-El-Haj in chartered planes before the black-and-white spotted cows died. It was a project financed by the Saudi judiciary's own funds and from subsidies from the World Food Programme.

The large Schleswig-Holstein animals, which produce a maximum milk yield, were used to the northern climate. They were relocated by air to a hot, sandy valley in the Saudi Arabian highlands on a trial basis. Air-conditioned stables were prepared. The animals never saw the southern daylight. The vet assumed they did not even know that they were no longer in Schleswig-Holstein. Hunziger doubted this, as animals perceive subtleties in the air, differences in magnetism, and can sense a foreign environment.

Judging by their appetite, one could see that the animals were confused. The planners and architects of the stables had ignored the notes on pages 84ff. of the files, as they had not been translated. Concentrated feed in cube form was stored in the adjoining rooms. This the animals ignored.

By the time Hunziger arrived, the breeding stock had three days to live, a few had laid down, lowing, their minders on the phone. The transport of any trusty hay from the Federal Republic of Germany was precluded by cost. At that point, it would have been more cost effective to allow the project to fail. Hunziger (12 days ago, even more determined than here in the castle hotel) decided to search in the region itself, flew off down the south-east coast of the peninsula, checked stockpiles in Kenya, Somalia, Egypt via radio. He found pressed bales in Ethiopia; a charter transport company run by young men in Kuwait.

The first bales arrived on Friday, they were torn apart and divided into the troughs. The cattle, probably the easternmost and southernmost breeding stock in Schleswig-Holstein, were saved as soon as they registered the familiar smell. They forgave being subjected to bunker life and supplied the Saudi upper class with milk in individual glasses at a price of $86 a go. Hunziger had slept little during the rescue operation. At the congress in Munich, Hunziger the saviour had to get involved in a hopeless dispute with the Belgian agricultural faction. These EC officials were in favour of the idea of an average breeding standard. They were regarded as participants in an INDUSTRIAL CONSPIRACY that wanted to reduce valuable regional domestic animal cultures to the concept of a standardised animal machine product in order to 'remove barriers to competition'.

## NEGLIGENCE IN WAR, NUCLEAR POWER AND THE DEATH PENALTY

### THE LIMITS OF HUMAN RIGHTS

As the head of the insurance department of a major company currently undergoing market losses due to its merger with a French corporation, Ariovist M. was speaking before a group of experts on the following topic: 'Human rights do not authorize three things: (1) the death penalty (2) war (3) the nuclear industry.'

Many other things, he says, are beyond collective regulation. These three examples, however, respond to 'ingrained negligence'. This negligence is a permanently effective force. Moreover, immediately after its constitution in 1789, humanity had killed its teacher, the king. Even if this individual king had made no effort to act as a teacher, by killing him humanity had destroyed the 'vessel' authorizing it to do extraordinary things. As far as the death penalty is concerned, Ariovist M. continued, no one could control the difference to public murder. Everything is carried out by proxy. None of those who do the killing are, in the event of error, prepared to accept responsibility for their role.

The second and third examples are even simpler: They concern HUMANITY'S OVERCONFIDENCE. Nobody can touch WAR or an ATOM with their fingers.

- Why are you supporting a king?
- You haven't understood the principle. It is not in the power of individuals or a populace to appoint a king. He is a teacher, as there is no proxy.
- You mean appointed by God?
- That is one possible interpretation. I myself am a pagan.
- But how do we reach this teacher?
- We decapitated him.
- We did not! The French were the ones to decapitate their king.
- . . . on humanity's behalf. We have to take credit for that.
- Therefore we should have also prevented the death of Christ the King?
- Most certainly. The one presupposes the other.
- You mean, without the death of Christ the King, the head of Louis XIV wouldn't have rolled?
- The one cannot take place without the other.
- Without Louis' death then, no death on the cross? More than a thousand years earlier?
- That is exactly what I am speaking about.

- I'll ask again: As a royalist, you assume historical repercussions? What happens influences all pasts?
- I am no royalist. I am a man of facts. You asked my opinion—I can only respond with what I think.
- We thank you for the conversation.

## THE BLIND AND THE INEXPERIENCED

> 'Get a move on, friend. Time is fleeting.
> It's dripping away from our lives.'
> *Arno Schmidt*

The bile operation on 6 January, which the clinic's pathologist criticized after it ended fatally for the patient, was the result of blindness in one of the chief surgeon's eyes. He could no longer see clearly. He therefore resolved to be particularly careful in any future cases.

During the operation on 20 January, during which another patient died, a sudden case of high blood pressure—perhaps because the doctor made so much more effort than on 6 January—also reduced the doctor's vision, this time in his other eye as well, so that after a few unsuccessful incisions he handed over the operation to his young, still-inexperienced assistant. The latter is said to have been overwhelmed, but no doctor was watching, and the nurses remained stubbornly silent, digging into the wound 'according to the textbook'. The patient died a horrible death.

Now the assistant doctor, the blind man and the supervisor of the two—the surgeon Zarborsky, who was on leave and did not know a thing about any visual impairments—have been charged with involuntary manslaughter.

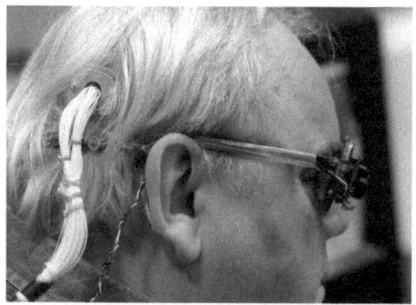

FIGURE 10. 'Camera electronically linked to the occipital lobe.' Interface between humans and technology. This allows the unsighted to see blurry, pale blue images.

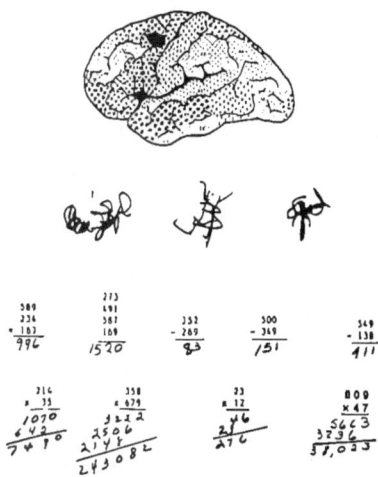

FIGURE 11. The history of *ratio*. When the mind can no longer think, says Jacques Derrida, it can still count. Following a small lesion in the left premotor cortex, the patient could no longer read or write any words, but could manage numbers in Arabic script. The scribbles show her attempts to write her name, the letters A and B, and the word *dog*. Her ability to write Arabic numbers remained unaffected.

## ENCOUNTER WITH THE UNKNOWN

Shortly after US Secretary of State Baker—who had recorded and accompanied the liquidation of the Soviet Union and the founding of the CIS like a notary public—had left, Dimitri W. from the Department for Unidentified Flying Objects in the KGB/Foreign Affairs, suspicious about the future of his position, was sitting opposite his counterpart from the CIA. The latter had travelled to Moscow to share experiences. A breakfast of caviar and salmon was served in the offices of what's referred to as the KGB tower. The CIA functionary opened the conversation.

- 96 per cent of all UFO phenomena are, according to your secret files, that is, those of the KGB, resolved, sorted according to 'natural causes and provocations, which, since 1951, the CIA has undertaken to cover up their own activities on Soviet soil'. Is that right?
- If anyone can confirm this, then that person is me.
- Yes, that surprised me earlier. You claim to know more than the CIA.
- This has to do with the overall view.
- How can I understand that?
- Only one's adversary is interested enough in knowing everything your organization is doing. The CIA is divided into departments. They seal off their knowledge from one another. This corresponds to the conspiratorial rule. We, however, explored EVERYTHING.
- And the head of the CIA? In your estimation?
- Doesn't have any time for the overall view. Thanks to his daily planner, he is cut off from knowledge.
- Is that not the case in every intelligence apparatus?

- Of course. That is the case in life. Only one's adversary has an image of the whole. You say, 'The CIA knows . . .', 'The CIA assumes . . .', 'Since 1951 the CIA . . .'—that is all an unrealistic use of grammar. Only one employee—or separately from him a spy and separately from this a team of evaluators—can be the subject. Grammatically speaking, there is no such thing as the 'CIA' as a whole. The organization only emerges from the situation maps of *our* investigation results, and there as a shadow outline, i.e. virtually, in our computers.
- And in the press as an object of public interest?
- A bogeyman.
- Isn't that a bit harsh?
- Where is the press supposed to be getting its information?
- From you, for example?
- That would be diversion. It would produce a picture, but not one that has anything to do with the object, that is, a realistic analysis of our adversary.
- Either way. You confirm that 96 per cent of UFO reports are considered resolved.
- Not by us.
- That's what I said.
- According to the CIA resolved. We reviewed only about 37 per cent.
- And did not find anything unreal?
- What makes you think that unidentified flying objects are unreal?

- I mean extraterrestrial. Coming from the cosmos.
- Or long at home on Earth! Interspecific, so to speak. The unexplained 4 per cent are enough for me.
- Now, on to your experience.
- I was flying from the Caucasus administration district, coming over the Caspian Sea. I was expecting disruption from the south. However, an elongated, black armoured flying object approached from the northeast and pushed against the side of my aircraft.
- You could see that through the bullseye?
- No, from the cockpit. A blackish metal, seven metres next to us.
- A U-2?
- Believe me, I can tell the difference between what I saw and the outer shell of any American construction. This blackish metal bulged like the body of a tadpole and was able to envelop our machine.
- As in swallow?
- Not me, the machine.
- It kept on flying within this tadpole's mouth?
- We were flying. I was observing the gauges.
- Your pilot?
- A nervous type. I said: 'Easy now.' We were surrounded by darkness. I said: 'Remember the phrase: "Thank God when He presses down upon you, and thank Him, when he lets go again",' just so that there would be a human tone in the cabin, so that something popularly understandable would loosen up the atmosphere.
- Weren't you afraid?

- What would that have helped?
- That's not the question when you're afraid.
- We were prepared for anything.
- But not for that.
- Not for that. It came unexpectedly.
- And after that you lost consciousness?
- I was still working on my watch.
- What does that mean?
- When we think we can no longer control a situation, we are to press on our watchband two times. This fixes the exact time of the blackout for subsequent investigations. It's something we practice.
- Do you know what happened after that?
- 16 hours must have gone by. I was in a hollow in the tundra. Pieces of my parachute nearby. My legs broken. The crash had been observed. Six hours later, I was found by the helicopter.
- They (whatever they were) had thrown you away?
- Inspected, i.e. operated on. Removed some parts, inserted spare parts (which worked, but which we were unable to analyse later). Then properly stitched up with sutures and wiring that were not subject to biological rejection, and then more or less carelessly thrown away.
- Very contradictory.
- Yes, first care, then none. Why sew it up, take care of spare parts, remove only one kidney? On the other hand, why keep something as unimportant as 2 metres of intestine? Why throw me away after trying to

preserve my life? The fatality rate of a parachute accident in the tundra is 86 per cent.

– Perhaps they knew that?
– Why are you saying 'they'? It is not certain that it had to do with people.
– But it cannot have been a diversion of the US (the American said).
– No, otherwise we'd know. And not because we need to identify a detail, but because we would have learnt about it as some kind of PLAN, when not to say RESULT, thanks to our moles. We cannot fully know what is happening on the planet. But what the CIA knows, that we read in full.
– Even Department 13's knowledge?
– The National Reconnaissance Office? That was always of great interest to us. We would have liked to know more about that.
– And then you reported back?
– Well, whatever I was able to reproduce: the missing organs, my clock. My subjective impressions before and after, not enough.
– Your overall verdict?
– That is a matter for the analysis team. It would be wrong for an observer to commit themselves.
– This was all two weeks before the collapse of the Soviet Union, that is, at the beginning of December 1991?
– Exactly. Our entire department was liquidated.
– Nevertheless, you were kept on standby.

- I received the 'unofficial advice' of my superiors (who had nothing more to command) to keep me ready as a kind of bait in case the 'aliens', the 'possible alien ally or enemy', came back into contact with me again. The preservation of my body after 'exploitation' could indicate that they wanted to renew contact. What if interfaces had been built into me?
- Nothing happened?
- Not until now. In the meantime, responsibilities have disintegrated.
- You said that at first your superiors were 'as if electrified'?
- As if they had expected such a thing. It turned out that in the early days of the revolution, on 18 August 1918, contact of a similar kind had taken place at the Bolshevik Workers' Division in Ustyurt. My superiors thought that the USSR could be saved by contact with extraterrestrials. When no other power in the world could save the empire. A delegation of unidentified flying objects would have been simplistic in this situation.
- How so?
- If the aliens had been hostile, all the forces in our country would have gathered around the government. I assume that the supreme command would have passed to the General of the Strategic Rocket Forces. That would have been a safe man for the Soviet Union.
- And so, violated by strangers, you would've become the empire's lifeline? Did Gorbachev know about that?

- All phone lines to headquarters were cut.
- Personal repercussions?
- None. My one kidney works as if it were two. The scarred seams made of strange plastic turn a bluish colour if it rains for more than two weeks.
- How many of the unexplained 4 per cent of UFO sightings are covered by your report?
- An unmeasurable quantity. Eventually 0.000827 per cent. An isolated incident. We'll learn more when I'm autopsied.
- Let's hope you have a long time to go before that!
- Let's hope so.
- Are you a curious individual?
- That is my profession.
- Your 'former' profession?
- No, no. One never changes that kind of profession.
- What would you rather have, a long life or being certain of how making contact with UFOS works?
- I do not answer hypothetical questions, not even to you. I'd be interested in contact with a third party.
- And if these creatures are 'inhuman'?
- They are definitely not human. Perhaps highly sensitive machines?
- Would you call the curiosity that I can read in your face compulsive?
- Occupational.

# LA VALSE DES GÉNÉRAUX.
# THE WALTZ OF THE GENERALS.

### A DESCRIPTION

>'At best, one is penalized
>for one's virtues.'

In the foreground, generals with untrained bodies trying to portray that they 'were ready'. They orient themselves on the assassin's car still heading straight for the minister's vehicles. The assassin was slumped over the wheel, he'd even pulled the key out of the ignition when he could no longer see anything and thought he had been shot.

His vehicle knocked over several coffins. The defence minister's bodyguard freezes for several seconds after his accurate shot. He breathes after the too-rapid shot, looking for orientation.

The generals, not trained as bodyguards, were photographed by the press in lively, anxious movement. The colonial army in Chad is disgraced.

Hernu, France's Defence Minister, stands there 'as if made of stone' (petrifié). In emergencies like that, his job is to remain still, so that photos suggest 'unshakeable calm'. There are three possibilities: the minister will either be run over, shot or blown to bits. Or he will manage to escape unscathed. Then it all depends on the first photo depicting the situation 'after the assassination attempt'. The best thing is for the minister to stand 'like a rock'. It doesn't look good if he tries to take cover from further shots.

In a press photo, anyone who moves and seeks orientation while still moving gives the impression of a clumsy dancer. The incident took place on the occasion of the funeral of a soldier recruited in Chad, whose death in the undeclared war had no identifiable cause. The family of the deceased was distraught. They hadn't slept. They were unable to find out why their brother, nephew or son had ended up in the enemy's minefield. Lionel Rahal, brother of the fallen recruit, the would-be assassin, wanted to act on the family's behalf. He wanted to give the non-commissioned officers a kind of shove from another motor vehicle, frighten the dignitaries, threaten the minister, bring the truth out of the authorities.

Such a short-sighted act is punishable by law. The assassin's mother, having lost one son in Chad (which is the occasion of the state funeral), throws herself on her second son, the assassin, who has just been lifted out of the car. She throws herself over the man lying on the ground, the 'corpse'. The medics from the base arrive immediately afterwards. The dead man stirs. The woman is carefully separated from her son's body, while a relative attacks the minister's bodyguard—the one who shot the family member and stopped the assassination vehicle—with his fists. Which results in powerful photos.

If all the assassin's family members were now to fall at the feet of the minister, who stands there 'like a rock' until he is called away, and beg for a swift act of mercy, it would hardly be possible for the prosecutors to press for the assassin to be punished. A grandiose public appearance by the minister with another photo!

Interview of the correspondents from *Le Monde* with the Minister.

    MINISTER: I am indeed thankful.

    CORRESPONDENT: What do you mean thankful, you can be jolly glad, Minister!

    MINISTER: Well, I am. Tell that to the bodyguard who saved me with his presence of mind.

CORRESPONDENT: He will surely ask what's to come of him.

MINISTER: Nothing. He will be transferred.

CORRESPONDENT: Is that not somewhat unthankful?

MINISTER: Public opinion, as you know, will not tolerate the defence minister having successful bodyguards.

Shortly thereafter a conversation with the correspondents from *Le Figaro*.

CORRESPONDENT: People will not find it particularly appreciative of you to transfer the man who saved your life to the middle of nowhere, Minister.

MINISTER: What should I do?

CORRESPONDENT: Prepare to honour him.

MINISTER: He will be honoured!

CORRESPONDENT: Confirm him in his post and perhaps replace him next year.

MINISTER: That won't work.

CORRESPONDENT: In future, bodyguards will think twice about whom they protect. If they're successful, they'll be penalized.

MINISTER: The public sphere will not tolerate my having a good bodyguard by my side.

CORRESPONDENT: Had he not shot at all or missed, you would now be dead.

MINISTER: Well, then he would be transferred anyway.

CORRESPONDENT: A thankless job.

MINISTER: One doesn't shoot at ministers.

During the assassination attempt, the minister's two aides, like the others present, including 16 commanding generals, had run around, turning to expose only their bodies' narrow sides to bullets, even though the assassin had used a vehicle and only the bodyguards had fired. This is why the aides tried to show some composure afterwards.

- The minister cannot tolerate having a bodyguard around. This is a dictate of public opinion, which rejects the idea of ministers protecting themselves while ordinary soldiers in Chad walk unprotected onto mines. The funeral was the cause of the accident.
- In an undeclared war . . .
- That's right. The bodyguard must be transferred. But that will be interpreted as ingratitude on the part of the minister.
- Had the minister died, and had it been proven that no bodyguard could have protected him, the bodyguard would have kept his position.
- So that there remains a chance for him to be shot, too? Equal opportunities between assassins, ministers and bodyguards?
- I would put it differently: ungrateful ministers are shot. What does the reader want?
- The world to be a fair place.

The difficulties were the result of a balance sheet (total account). The press photos remained negative for the generals who accompanied the minister and looked like hopping hares. The presence of too small a contingent of French troops in Chad was unpatriotic.

The occasion, the honouring of a single local non-commissioned officer with a state funeral, without the family having been informed, was the result of poor planning. The successful bodyguard had to bear the costs.

## A 570-MILLION-YEAR-OLD CLOAK OF INVISIBILITY

For 570 million years, coexistence between sea sponges and bacteria. Sea sponges seem to carry the bacteria as an 'inner heritage' of their forebears. Wilkinson found the bacteria in 296 sponges in the Mediterranean, the Red Sea, the south coast of England near Plymouth and along the Great Barrier Reef in Australia. Immunologically speaking, close affinity between bacterial strains. The bacteria colonised an ancestor of the sponges in the Precambrian age.

The sponges feed on bacteria. They filter out the non-symbionts from a mixture of bacteria. These are the only things they consume. The sponges use a kind of immune system to distinguish between their own and foreign bacteria. It is likely that the micro-organisms conceal their bacterial nature from the sponges by means of a special capsule that encases them, so that they are not recognised as food. A 570-million-year-old cloak of invisibility.[21]

---

21 The strangest thing, however, Wilkinson writes, is that this phenomenon apparently originated in the Cambrian period in six different places on earth which have no connection to one another. This cloak of invisibility was designed six times. With minimal differences. If we transport sponges (which nature cannot do) in tank containers by plane from the Great Barrier Reef to Plymouth, the sponges there will also eat the protected bacteria out of the imported Australian sponges.

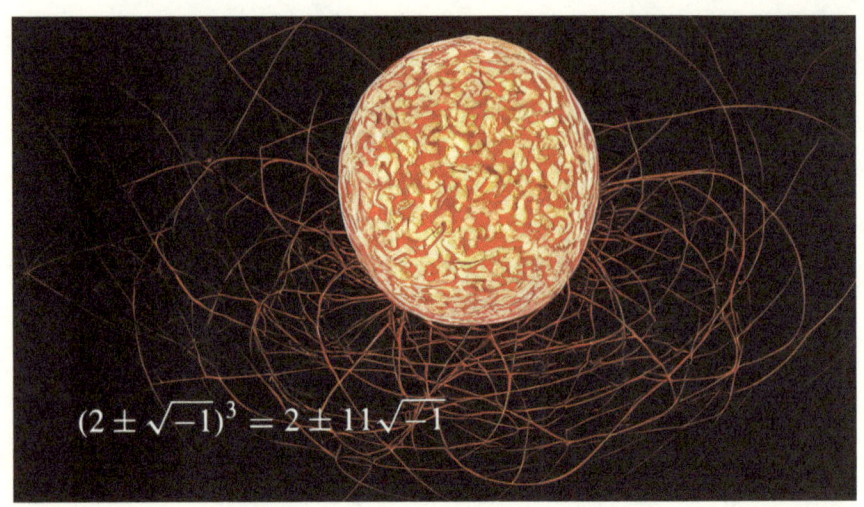

FIGURE 12. 'With cross-linking'. Micro-organism, shortly before 670 million years ago. 'Intelligent prehistorical cell . . .'

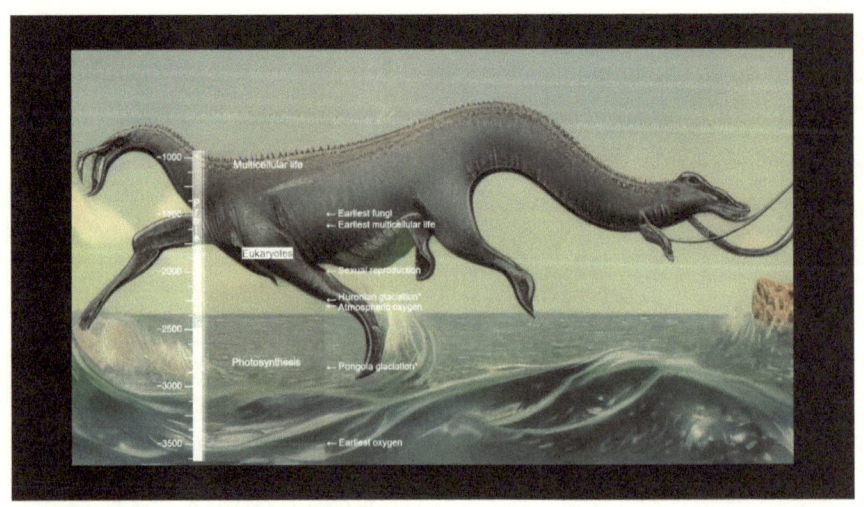

FIGURE 13. An extinct two-headed ancestor.

FIGURE 14. 'From nature's past'.

## ROBINSON IN RUSSIA

The latest findings are concentrated in the ruins of what was once Russia's largest research institution. These ruins are tolerant rooms. Whoever is incapable of holding out in the US can save themselves by going to the Robinson Islands of Russia, Leonard Shlain maintains.

Through a dirt-encrusted window, he looks out onto Moscow's Garden Ring, an urban ring road. But that is not what he's interested in. He is paying attention to the seven monitors showing the dwarf-like world of his new experimental set-ups in extreme close-up.[22]

The billionaire Berezovsky is financing Leonard Shlain's research with 0.006 per cent of the proceeds of the television stations he has established, a kind of river or stream which, like the Volga in Lenin's time, yields profits from which the internationalist struggle can be financed. To this end, companies capable of being listed on the stock exchange were set up on the Caribbean islands.

Shlain's secret is anti-alchemical. He is uninterested in either the homunculus or a magical substance that will turn people into Superman. He is looking for the key with which he can access the information that people's bodies carry around with them throughout their lives by virtue of evolution. How much knowledge is contained in the constellation of 11 or 23 molecules in the liver or kidneys, of which no brain knows a thing! This is life's black market! Shlain rummages through it by pushing his chips forward like detectives. All that we need from people for this research, Shlain

---

22 J. C. Polkinghorne describes in *The Quantum World* (London, 1924) a series of incredible quantum experiments. They influence the nanoscale, i.e. atoms and even electrons unexpectedly turn out to be 'excited' or 'enthusiastic'. These phenomena can be measured in the micro range. As they oscillate between two incompatible realities, two different universes, they can only be inferred from their consequences.

says, is punctuality: a few cells here, a few interfaces there providing access to the treasure trove of HUMAN PASTS, a Nibelung treasure. We'll be ready in 12 years. That's what he told Berezovsky, and the POWERFUL ONE accepted it as such.[23]

ADDENDUM

Leonard Shlain's specific assumption: With the means of mainstream biology and genetic engineering, we barely get as far as the atom; that is where understanding ends. Because we have distanced ourselves from this mainstream, we are known, Shlain says, as Robinsons. I myself, he continues, was instructed with the experiments of W. Brand and N. Schlitz and am familiar with those of Jacobo Grinberg-Zylberbaum (*Subtile Energies*, Vol. 3, 1993). We apply psychokinetic and electrodermal activity, together with morphic gravitation, to the most interesting interface between the *known* and the *unknown*. Leibniz calls this the separatrix. We do this, Shlain adds, according to the rules of quantum physics and with biological data. Henceforth the measurements *jump*. VIRTUAL and REAL alternate with each other. This is the genesis of the SPIRIT. On this basis we employ the theories of Alfonso Rueda and H. E. Putthoff: *BEYOND $E = mc^2$*.

---

23 Twelve years, Shlain says, are, according to the ideas of the Berlin Republic, not an extended period. In terms of the Third Reich, however, 12 years mark the difference between life and death. No information, no exodus without a long memory.

The project of a parallel humanity, Shlain adds, cannot be expressed in annual figures (in discussion with Berezovsky I talk about financial plans and thereby dates; biologically speaking, such dates are unreal). I can only describe the biological and educational processes that ensure the emancipation of the new particles we are working on, i.e. the constitution of a DIVERSE EVOLUTION, in terms of millennia, indeed in groups of 10,000 years each. I am not entirely sure that this can happen without civil war.

FIGURE 15. Alfonso Rueda and H. E. Puthoff. Their study INERTIA AS A ZERO-POINT-FIELD LORENTZ FORCE is considered groundbreaking.

## THE QUANTUM VACUUM, A POETIC METAPHOR

'Poetry is all that is really Real.'

*Novalis*

René N. Schlitz received one of the literary detectives of a large German daily in his laboratory's canteen. The quantum expert was dumbfounded by the unexpected literary interest in his texts, which have also been published in German. He welcomed the fact that the content of his research was now also finding its way into the *feuilleton* pages.[24]

- You received this year's Georg Büchner Prize for a biophysical manuscript. That seems rather unusual.
- But it's a fact.
- What is a quantum vacuum?

---

[24] In fact, he traced the vocabulary he used back to the German philosopher Schelling's theory of nature. That had been the last approach to conceptualizing natural science in language. But how does one express in words the dizzying energy density of 10 multiplied by 94 Gev/cm³ in mass-energy equivalence? That is more than the total amount of matter in the universe in a small space! The observable universe, however, floats, so to speak, on the surface of an ocean that has this density.

- It is the lowest possible state of energy in a system in which both the equations of quantum mechanics and those of the special theory of relativity are valid. It is the so-called ZERO-POINT FIELD.
- And that, you write, is an 'immeasurable ocean of energy, which lets the particles of matter emerge like dolphins from the depths in the form of substructures'?
- Well, if dolphins were indeed like electrons or protons.
- Is the poetic form of expression you prefer as a physicist misleading?
- Not at all. Actually, the contemplation of nature alone is poetic.
- And how is the 'Dirac sea' an ocean of electrons with negative energy?
- That is a case of 'pair-production'.
- Sounds like a novel.
- One can say that the observable universe arises out of the quantum vacuum. The zero-point vacuum 'becomes explosively unstable and splits into MATTER and GRAVITATION'. In the less turbulent Robertson-Walker phase, this huge energy field synthesizes into matter as we know it.
- And so you are materialistic?
- What does that mean?
- Another tea?
- Gladly.

## MY PATERNAL ANCESTORS

As the trademark of their products, they chose three arrows, one pointing right, one left and one upwards. They attached the name *Prudens*, in German translation: Kluge. They survived the Peasants' War thanks to camouflage or to their remaining neutral.

In the eighteenth century, the clan practised LARGE FORMS OF CLOCKMAKING. They repaired or constructed clocks for church spires, hence 'large forms'. They survived the Thirty Years' War in hardship and with losses. How many of them were there at the beginning, how few at the end! They are interrelated with emigrants from France who emigrated for religious reasons. These generations wander through the nineteenth century. The one forebear I myself saw would set his personal watch every day at 11 a.m. according to the large clock of the St Martini church, even though it was not one of the family's.

## A COMPLICATED GENERATIONAL SEQUENCE

The tribune Constantius Chlorus ('the pale'), in charge of the legionnaires in Asia Minor and Syria, went into an inn somewhere in today's Anatolia. He ordered a glass of wine. It was brought to him by a sturdy, attractive girl. One glance was all it took for both. The commander negotiated with the innkeeper, the girl's father. He allowed the young woman, whose name was Helena, to sit on his war steed. The two never parted again.

Constantius Chlorus was appointed Caesar of the Western Empire by Emperor Diocletian. The condition was that he marry a princess of the imperial house. After consulting with Helena, Constantius Chlorus married Theodora and even became somewhat accustomed to his attractive high-ranking wife with whom he had three sons and two daughters. In his mind, however, he remained faithful to Helena, to whom he owed his son Constantine.

This son was born out of wedlock, grew up, as far as the empire went, without rank. Later, he became known as CONSTANTINE THE GREAT who, not being religious himself, opened the Roman Empire to Christianity and subsequently granted his mother Helena the status of empress, so that at least her sarcophagus, now preserved in the Vatican vaults, would receive an immeasurable rank.

There was never another emperor whose work remained as uncontested as that of CONSTANTINE THE GREAT. Which, however, did not help any of his descendants all that much. In just a few years, all his sons were murdered.

As chance would have it, an imperial grandson was mistaken for the son of a servant girl at birth. The maid travelled back to her homeland, which is near present-day Niš. From there, anonymously but with the emperor's genes, a line of farmers and later innkeepers developed until 1850. Four of those sons emigrated to Chicago. A great-grandson of the immigrants, living in Silicon Valley, developed a chip that used living brain cells to control a magnificent 40 cm$^3$ device, a huge object of nanotechnology. For this interface between a human organ and electronics, this descendant, whose name (according to his birth certificate) was Nikos Koulisses Athanassoulas but who called himself Nicky Kaylos, acquired a European, a British and a US patent.

Then he died. The patent and associated product—namely, a functioning interface between life and dead matter—still lie in the cellar of a building 40 kilometres from San Francisco on the beach of an ocean bay. One last heir to the lineage and temperament of Helena and Constantius Chlorus is still missing, and it is he who finds the artefact in the cellar and uses it to set a parallel line to humanity in motion.

## THINKING ABOUT ONE'S OWN CHILDREN IN 1908

He was from Westphalia. She came from a small village only 20 kilometres away from where he was born. The route from blacksmith's apprentice to railway-line owner took 12 years. In 1908, twins by the names of Ernst and Friedrich were baptised.

The couple knew knew little about their forebears. They were anonymous. The two parents from 1908, they realized as they emptied glasses of wine punch at dusk, would not have been there had they not had ancestors as far back as the protozoa. Emotionally, they tried to keep the safety of their offspring in mind.

Bernd Schwietzke set up a foundation whose aim was to ensure the security of the coming decades, contrary to the armaments programme of the German Navy League, and even to guarantee it with the foundation's funds. Obviously, Xaver Holtzmann writes, his means (Schwietzke was only a millionaire) were too slender.

In the Second World War, both of the Schwietzkes' sons died at the front.

FIGURE 16. Official agency photo of general mobilization for the German Reich, 1914.

FIGURE 17. Fourteen days later, the corporal looking into the camera at bottom left is dead. The young boy on the right in the Schiebermütze (i.e. 'flat cap'—in 1914, the German expression is still unknown) died in 1941 in the air raid on Rostow. The reasons behind 'his' world war are laid on 1 August 1914.

## HOW THE WAR WAS LOST

In January 1917, so-called headquarters are housed in Pless Castle, near the Polish border. 300 civil-servant rooms, the officers therein. There are three moods: (1) depression (2) a determined will to persevere (3) the narrowing of all thoughts, narrow-mindedness.

Snow covers the manicured English lawn. Leaden grey the sky. The chancellor drives up the long avenue between bare trees to the palace, nervously smoking cigarettes. Now he enters the huge hall whose walls are decorated with hunting trophies, climbs the marble staircase and is led into the conference room which was created by the redecoration of a dining room. Here the Field Marshal (Hindenburg), the Quartermaster General (Ludendorff), the Chief of the Admiral's Staff (Holtzendorff) and the three heads of the Kaiser's cabinet are waiting; the Kaiser is informed that the meeting is about to begin.

The FEELING of all the people in this room is exasperation. The Quartermaster General (a demonic person whose willpower usually tries to occupy the people sitting next to him at table) is depressed by the excessive tension of the autumn and winter days. The occupier has occupied himself. The KAISER: impatient, unready to listen to himself or others; he wants to leave. The three cabinet chiefs: infected by the Kaiser's non-presence. These people have ALREADY BEEN THERE TOO LONG. The imperial chancellor has NOT BEEN THERE LONG ENOUGH. His feelings, tired out, lie torn between Berlin and the Pless Castle driveway. They were shaken on the train. It is in this emotional state that the decision to open the 'unlimited submarine war' is taken and, as a result, the US is drawn into the First World War.

He is not immune from the terrible wrongness of the decision forcing its way into his consciousness. After the imperial chancellor has agreed (everyone leaves the room), he sits at the window and looks out over the frozen pond in the park.

He runs a hand through his short grey hair. In his throat he feels something like thickened spittle or mucus. Perhaps he's caught a cold. Of course, he says, IF success beckons, we must act ACCORDINGLY. He didn't emphasize the IF, but says that the IF is decisive. Herr von Reischach, a court official, walks up to him, which is why Bethmann Hollweg had spoken. 'What is it?' von Reischach asks. 'Have we lost a battle?' 'No,' Bethmann Hollweg replies, 'but this is the FINIS GERMANIAE.' Herr von Reischach says: 'You should step down.' The imperial chancellor shakes his head. 'As an officer, you have to follow the orders of your superiors, even if you disagree with them.' But the imperial chancellor is the supreme superior. Following this exchange Herr von Reischach too believed the war was lost. The expression END OF GERMANY (but there are as few such endings as there are Germanies) was making the rounds, had damaged the chancellor's authority. From then on, he was considered feeble.

## THE INVENTOR OF INFILTRATION TACTICS

The man frequently credited as being the inventor of so-called infiltration tactics was named Oskar von Hutier. Commander of the German 8th Army, which conducted the 1917 offensive against Riga. Hutier's henchmen carried out the only poison-gas attack that was a resounding success. 'For the first time, German weapons benefited from the fact that they could be used in the direction of the western current of the weather.' The Germans broke through the Russian front; their blind enemies, to the degree they could still breathe, were incapable of reassembling. Von Hutier still had 16,000 tonnes of poison gas leftover.

FIGURE 18. Oskar von Hutier, 1917.

## '... LIKE A MULTITUDE OF SOFT WHISTLES...'

On the evening of 22 June 1916, Lieutenant Bechu of the 130th Division staff sat down to dinner with his general in the command post near Souville. It was a calm summer night. Suddenly, all the German guns fell silent. For the first time in days, there was complete silence. The officers gave each other worried looks, because, said Bechu, 'a man fears not battle, but a trap.'

After a number of minutes, they could hear a sound in the air 'like a multitude of soft whistles, following one after another, without cease, like thousands upon thousands of birds flying at a furious pace, slicing the air, rushing towards our heads'.

A sergeant ran into the dugout without knocking: *Mon general*, grenades above us, thousands of grenades that won't explode!

Come on, let's have a look, the general replied.

As the three of them stood outside listening, a 'pungent, nauseating odour of decay, similar to the smell of stale vinegar' crept out of the ravine. Before Verdun, the German forces had been provided with a valuable new invention: phosgene, also known as 'green cross' gas due to the marking on the shells. The gas curtain over the French artillery did not dissipate in the windless night. The artillerymen quickly donned their gas masks and ran to the guns in order to be ready. Nothing saved them from suffocation; in some horrible way, the gas penetrated the gas masks they were wearing. Now the problem for the higher command was to find a crew to move the piles of bodies away from the guns into the bushes or ravines; the command assumed that any replacements that found their fellow soldiers lying in heaps would not be ready or technically skilful enough to fight. There was complicated technical equipment to operate, the guns. As the curtain of gas refused to lift, shovel crews to remove the dead could not be brought forward during the night. 'The only good thing was that for a while the flies that were everywhere on the polluted battlefield disappeared.' Again and again, doctors grabbed their throats and fell over.

The German command did not utilize the effects of the gas bombardment. The gas tended to settle in depressions, leaving the French batteries in high positions *relatively unscathed*. The Chief of Staff of the German 5th Army had not relied on the phosgene alone either. The artillery was therefore ordered to stop firing gas four hours before the infantry attack and to 'follow up with normal ammunition'. This bombardment with explosive shells created the air movement that dispersed the gas. At least a few piles of dead could be removed from sight on the French side. Reserves rushed up to occupy the guns.

## A FORGOTTEN WEAPON

### THE ONLY FORM OF EFFECTIVE DISARMAMENT IS CALLED FORGETTING

In a cellar near Antwerp, the liquidator winding up the assets of an insolvent electronics group (formerly a shipping company) found a batch of old poison-gas shells. The book value was assessed at $21 million USD. They were one of a kind. Nowhere in the world were there still factories that could produce or even repair such goods. Nor were there any buyers on the world market. Just as there were no guns capable of firing these bullets, coated with valuable alloys. Enquiries on the GREY MARKET—that is, the unofficial, typically covert arms trade—revealed 'no interest'.

According to the liquidator, no young people at the war colleges are interested in chemical warfare any more. The knowledge has migrated to civilian warfare against vermin. The use of poison gas to kill civilians also seems to have been abandoned. The execution centres in the US, which keep poison gas ready for execution, only require small quantities. Here, too, there is a lack of engineering expertise for practical application.

That wasn't the case in 1936, the 86-year-old weapons dealer added. The entrepreneur I learnt from sold another batch to North Africa. Beginning in 1929, those high-quality warfare agents of 1916 were replaced by rapidly producible, fast-acting *nerve agents*. The Antwerp liquidator noted that the high book value of the combat-gas stocks in the cellars of the bankrupt company was the result of reports by air-force experts who had advocated the conversion of artillery shells into bombs in 1926; the intention was to gas people in city centres in the event of a war by aerial attack. Keeping the chemical aerosol, which was difficult to control, close to the ground proved to be a problem.

A stockpile of weapons which had fallen into oblivion!

The liquidator could not have the cellar cleared because no one knew how to dispose of the material. Hence it was more advantageous to leave a valuation in the books that justified continuing to pay the rent for the space while leaving open the question of whether it was scrap, a treasure for future use or a case of damage.

## THE FIFTH ART OF FORGETTING

It all started with his forgetting of names. He could no longer say what had taken place over the last year. Had anything worth mentioning, worth remembering happened at all?

Early in the morning, he felt, as per his usual, electrified. During the night, he had forgotten. He drove 67 km on rural roads, where the challenge was to avoid accidents. The moment was what counted. He felt something when he moved intensely, or in a roundabout way, or skilfully, or otherwise functionally or violently.

He had had himself examined. The doctor told him that none of the organic causes of memory loss could be verified. A psychoanalyst he consulted reassured him that, what with all his knowledge of the human soul, he could say that none of the examples of the man's forgetting were based on repression. The man's ability to remember also returned at irregular intervals. 'France's third Prime Minister after Edgar Faure and Mendès-France was named Guy Mollet.' For weeks, he could see the man's face in his mind's eye but could not remember the name. No one asked him about it. In this respect, whether he remembered or not didn't affect his business whatsoever. He needed the information for his sense of self. It irritated him that at times this trace no longer counted among the clamour of associations.

- You have to understand that many of your memories are lying beneath a heap of junk. Buried beneath rubble.
- And that's not pathological? It's not irreversible?
- It is based on overlay. You can create such INTERFERENCE even with electrical current.
- It unsettles me because it limits my room for manoeuvring. Suddenly, on the phone, I don't know what it is I wanted to say.
- It's the fifth art of forgetting. All the various pieces of information become too similar to one another.
- They pile up?
- Not even. They form a white smoke.
- Is that why I feel good at the moment?
- Yes, and a past emerges from it.
- Then certainly I must remember something earlier, something unmistakeable?
- No. The smoke of the FIFTH FORGETTING is quite substantial. I believe that experiences that were not different from one another in your memory and that were important to you at the time you experienced them now form a block. They trigger bodily reactions.
- Yes, I sweat. After a talk on the phone or a dangerous fax, my armpits stink.
- You see? That is substantial. In terms of your traditional memory, it is useless. You would have to keep a diary. Or an electronic notebook, and every half hour or so, dictate what you are doing or believe you have experienced.

- I can remember all that.
- But not in your head.
- I don't?
- It superimposes itself in one's power of recall. Presence of mind erases our yesterdays.
- What's it comparable to?
- A tiger-attack. The present devours the present.
- So this FIFTH ART OF FORGETTING is a kind of characteristic of the new human being?
- This is precisely what I am trying to explain to you.
- Should I be concerned?
- Very.
- A decline that I cannot afford in my job? On the outside it can mimic Alzheimer's?
- I am not here to give you advice. I am here to give you an expensive diagnosis.
- What can I do?
- Change professions!

My talk with the analyst did little to console me. There is a new year before me. Perhaps my death will come before my deficit becomes known.[25]

---

25 The mechanism, F., the experienced analyst and still-orthodox Freudian, said, cannot be met with the depth dimension of psychoanalysis. It has to do with a very superficial circuit that, if there were such a thing, would be found in chapter 4 of *The Psychoanalytic Primer*. An intriguing libido does not erase a day, but rather other zones of memory by proxy according to a roll of the dice, 'in the same way one takes revenge', so to speak. My colleagues in anatomy and we analysts, F. continued, puzzle over some patients for a long time

## THE POWER OF FATE

Just after Christmas 1938, British Prime Minister Chamberlain appears in the box of the Royal Opera House in Rome, on the far left. Next to him is Prime Minister Mussolini. Next to him, standing tall, is Head of the Foreign Office, Lord Halifax, with Italian Foreign Minister Count Ciano on the far right. Giuseppe Verdi's opera *The Power of Fate* (*La forza del destino*) is performed. Five years later, Count Ciano, Mussolini's son-in-law, will be shot by the latter.

Christmas and January have passed for the ageing Chamberlain in London and Rome. He attempts to *mediate*. He is unsure whether he understands what is involved in each case. Regarding Hitler he says: 'He either has to die, go to St Helena or become an architect in some office or other, preferably in some kind of "home".'

- You are saying that neither the British prime minister nor the Italian prime minister allowed themselves to be influenced by the opera because they had been brought up as RATIONALISTS. That is, they would not have had the strength to hinder the outbreak of war in September 1939 because they possessed too little of an opera-like power of imagination. In simple terms. Is this correct?
- That does sound simplified. Contracted into a single sentence as you've done here.
- Extended or rolled out in a hundred sentences, what are you trying to say?
- I do not express myself in film via sentences, but image sequences.

---

before we find out whether it is a case of early Alzheimer's or indeed the FIFTH ART OF FORGETTING.

- OK. Less subtly: is your view correct or not?
- That is up to the viewers to judge.
- But they don't do that!
- You are displaying the typical inferiority complex that public institutions have. The viewers most certainly do judge whether something is historically correct or not.
- Then if you could please repeat your thesis.
- That's not how things work . . .
- You claim that people who are unreceptive to the shock of a great tragedy, such as *Macbeth*, say, do not have the power to intervene in reality. No power of imagination—no action. Is that right?
- More or less.
- The four statemen who appeared in the opera loge didn't believe in witches. Is this why they themselves cannot practice witchcraft when things get serious?
- Put in simple terms.
- So you also deny Hitler's eyes their fascination?
- Certainly. His eyes were a dull grey. That is often the case. No sorcerer has eyes like that, if that's what you mean. There are books about it. He doesn't even appear in my film.
- Right after Christmas 1938, the British prime minister goes to Rome.
- Correct.
- With an umbrella.

- You saw it yourself. He is carrying an umbrella and wearing a dark coat. And a hat, like any decently dressed Englishman from the business district.
- But it wasn't raining in Rome?
- You have a strange idea of Italy in January.
- So it was?
- The clouds moved from North Africa over Sicily and on towards Rome. It was not raining. There was the risk of showers.
- Joking aside: The British prime minister was interested in peace?
- In making the necessary preparations.
- At his side, I see Mussolini, Count Ciano, Lord Halifax.
- Lord Halifax is Foreign Secretary. Former Viceroy of India. Count Ciano is Italy's foreign minister.
- And what are all these opera lovers in this loge going to do afterwards?
- That's the problem. All day long parades, now opera. They're not really working.
- How long does the opera last?
- Three and a half hours with an intermission.
- Which takes away from the time for political work.
- Not to mention the receptions, city tours, parades.
- So how much time is left for political work?
- From the four-day visit? 3 hours, 20 minutes.
- What did those in charge do all that time?
- It is difficult to understand without interpreters.

The *Neue Zürcher Zeitung* correspondent in Rome was interviewing the filmmaker Christian D., whose film about German East Africa was honoured with one of the highest awards in Canada. D. was calling his latest project 'News with Music'.

'Do you mean,' the NZZ correspondent asked, 'that the daily news should be accompanied by music?' Why not? Christian D. replied. This aroused the correspondent's curiosity and prompted further questions, which eventually led to THE POWER OF FATE of January 1939. No doubt, D. said, Chamberlain's attempts, supported by the able Lord Halifax, would have had an objective chance of blocking the outbreak of war in September 1939. For a moment, the key lay in Rome. Something like that can only be realized with music.

FIGURE 19. The power of fate, 1963. Death of Kennedy.

Contact sheet of a Christmas visit of the British foreign minister Halifax in Rome, who is supposed to prevent the outbreak of the Second World War. Fifth picture from the top, on the left: Halifax and Mussolini at the opera in Rome. They are attending a performance of Verdi's *La forza del destino*. To the right: Count Ciano, Italy's own foreign minister, who will be shot by Mussolini, his father-in-law (second from the left in the loge).

Contact sheet. Around the end of the First World War, members of the socialist left-wing opposition gather in secret in neutral Switzerland. This is the 'Zimmerwald Conference', the core of the Third Internationale, the only radical anti-war movement in the twentieth century and one of the core cells of the Russian Revolution of 1917. In the second image of the first contact sheet and in the last image of the second: Lenin. Second top-right image in the second contact sheet: Leo Trotsky.

FIGURE 20. Eugen Leviné and his wife Rosa with their son Genia, furlough 1916. Eugen Leviné, one of the most determined anti-war campaigners from the Socialist Internationale known as the Kienthaler Circle, was murdered by soldiers from a rightwing Bavarian Freikorps group in the courtyard of a Munich prison after they had put down the Bavarian Soviet Republic. His child was three years old.

## EXTREME DWARVES

'Critics assume the system will remain static forever. We've never assumed it would never change. We can play the countermeasure-counter-countermeasure game. In 16 years, the project will be less risky.'
*General Kadish,*
*Ballistic Missile Defense Organization (BMDO)*

- To what degree can you keep your new recruits, the nanocomputers, under control, General?
- Almost completely.
- And if they escape into the wild from your laboratories, or the weapons in which they've been embedded? As we know, a weapon can become stranded.
- Well, we will come up with countermeasures.
- And if the escaped nanobots enact countermeasures themselves, General?
- Then the familiar game begins: countermeasure for countermeasure. That's how we've been learning for 80 years.
- Nanobots are intelligent?
- Small and particularly intelligent.
- Invisible?
- Practically speaking, yes.
- They say that in evolution, the advantage is always on the side of the small organisms.
- They're machines.

- But as intelligences: rather lifelike?
- They are. Above all, in a network.
- Are they SELF-SUFFICIENT SYSTEMS?
- Most certainly.
- If they escape from you, what on earth will you be able to do? Until now, each and every self-sustaining system has found a way to reproduce.
- How are they supposed to do that? They don't have any sex.
- Are they capable of learning?
- Very much so.
- Social?
- They like one another, if that's what you mean. They like to be in company. The fact that they are sociable is the reason we can get them to achieve these things (and still reduce them to such dimensions). What I have learnt from this: intelligence does not come from logic, but sociability.
- Then these hybrid creatures, General, will certainly find a way to reproduce?
- Not in a laboratory and not in a space weapon!
- Could they survive in the cold of outer space?
- They could.
- Are they sensitive to heat?
- The latest models aren't.
- In the event of their escape, what is to be said against their setting in motion their own republics, a separate

evolution alongside that of humanity? Could they attach slaves or helpers to themselves?
- Not slaves, but automatons.
- Older generation robots?
- All those that are bigger than they are.
- Would your creations do something like that?
- They would betray themselves if they strengthened themselves in this way. That would provoke countermeasures from our side. They are too intelligent to take such a step and would postpone it for the time being. We are talking hypothetically here. I told you that this is a secret area.
- You did. How would one even notice that they had escaped and reproduced? That a second civilization of nanobots was overtaking us in the nano realm?
- A slow increase in the planet's temperature.
- Average earth temperature?
- On average and in those patches where they were concentrated.
- And if they are unclever enough to build groups?
- They are not unclever.
- Could there be other reasons for an average, gradual increase in the planet's temperature?
- Therein lies our problem.
- You can't see the nanos?
- Not outside the laboratory. You need devices to hold the nanos in an observable place if you want to 'see' or measure them.

- Invisible to the human eye?
- A human eye wouldn't be able to see a nanobot even under a microscope.
- The heat radiation alone gives them away? They can't stop from working?
- You could recognize them by what they arrange.
- When it is reported to the president of the United States that they have established themselves on Earth, how many are we talking about?
- A few million trillion.
- And you don't see that as dangerous?
- It's a secret project and cannot be discussed. In 16 years, it'll be less dangerous because we'll have countermeasures that also take into account (hypothetical, classified as secret) cases of leakage.
- And if that happens earlier?
- We need the nanobots.
- For the hit-to-kill-interceptor, the successor to the 59 kg wonder (137 cm long) from Raytheon in Tucson, Arizona?
- We have to trim the projectile to a size of 8 mm and a speed of 90 miles/sec. Engineers can't do that, only the nanos themselves can. This is how we protect the country against attacks from 'rogue states', if you'll pardon the expression (which we no longer use today).
- Where do you get your confidence that this will go well, General?
- I don't have any such confidence.

- Before the Senate committee, you spoke about confidence.
- That's an institutional term. Without confidence a project like ours couldn't be carried out. This has nothing to do with a personal illusion of my own.

The informal discussion took place in a bar near the Capitol where journalists and people from the Pentagon often got together; meeting in that public space wasn't considered suspect: an accredited place for non-conversations. The reporter from *The Washington Post* had noticed a movement in the Pentagon's budgets, which tied the nanobots project to the National Missile Defense (NMD) project. Together with his counterpart, he sought a loophole in the oath of secrecy without jeopardizing his career.

To that degree his interlocutor was a kind of hybrid, having exchanged an influential position in the Pentagon for one in one of the large foundations. He was speaking both as a man with a security clearance and as a private individual. If you stood up from the cosy seating area where they were busy exchanging speech and counter-speech and walked 7 metres to a circular window at head height, you would be able to see the distant Washington Monument, the ponds and the consistency of the lawn on the generously laid-out perspective leading away from the Capitol. Samuel B. Kippner, the retired general and lobbyist, was not irrational.

- It seems to me (the journalist said, who was positively touched by the affection with which Kippner had spoken of his 'invisible creatures') that every 10 years or so a crisis scenario becomes a thing, the death of the West or the end of civilization or what-have-you. But up until now no such fiasco has ever come to be.

May I ask you, Samuel, something personal? You have two children, I have two children.
- Yeah?
- From a control point of view, it is unlikely that your project will bring any happiness. Does that reassure you?
- That's precisely why I went over to the foundation. I'm a lobbyist, Steve, but I do not respond to any orders. My fear that I spoke of earlier relates to the fact that I don't know what happens when something gets changed after so much previous input in a machine like the Pentagon (and the armaments processes in the world). You must not see it psychologically (as good will, guilt, etc.). The system has learnt from all previous mistakes. Not me.
- Speaking as a journalist: I don't want to be a Cassandra.
- As a lobbyist I am a professional optimist. That aside, I've noticed that I enjoy it when the horizon is a) indefinite, b) full of hope. The only ones of our ancestors that are left are those who looked at things trustingly when they were born.
- At birth a baby doesn't see a thing. Only after a few days...
- Look at their hands! Look at how dependant they are! Trust is there before the new arrivals see anything with their eyes.
- You were in Berkeley?
- Yes, in 1967.
- You don't lose it completely.
- Not as a perspective.

- And does your career as a lobbyist contradict that?
- Not at the moment.
- Not getting involved is a stance?
- Because it will be worse if we plan.
- This speaks very much in favour of our replacement by the nanobots.
- I didn't know that you were a cynic, Steve.
- And I'm not allowed to write anything about it?

They had grown closer to each other emotionally. But this did not change the rules that apply in Washington between the press and the administration (or those in proximity to it) whatsoever. In that sense, neither a reporter from *The Washington Post* nor a person with a security clearance in the Pentagon can jump out of the system. Dwarves of communication. In the event of an emergency, just such a contact can be decisive. With this feeling, they treated themselves to a Havana.

FIGURE 21. My maternal forebears were simple farmers.

FIGURE 22. Star wars.

## DEVILS HAVE A WAITING PERIOD

### DOES A PARALLEL HUMAN RACE STAND A CHANCE?

> 'Wherever arrogance of the intellect mates with the spiritual obsolete and archaic, there is the Devil's domain.'
>
> Thomas Mann,
> 'Germany and the Germans,'
> Speech from 1945

### I

When he wasn't lying to himself (which he only did when fatigue overwhelmed him), he had always believed in his star. In the long wait that preceded the breakthrough of perestroika, he always felt that all that waiting would lead to a breakthrough. He was destined for an EXCELLENT LIFE, his superior, academic member S. M. Troyanovsky, said: You are one of my best colleagues, and if you allow me, I will call you my student.

This was foreboding, even if it only came from the silly Troyanovsky. The scientific institute where N. Nikofeyev defended his advantages year after year possessed so-called laser trees, the largest Siberian-grown crystals in the world. The working group had special status and special funds. It accompanied Russia's 'Spring of Nations' by building up stocks. This particular spring was almost over. Another waiting period.

The next 'comrade' or 'Robinson' could be reached in Geneva, Massachusetts or Australia via existent networks, telephone, fax or the Internet.

The Republic of Waiting, i.e. the dammed-up state of science, transferred N. Nikofeyev to Belarus. The location of secret, deregulated laboratories. On one occasion, a parliamentary control mission travelled there, asked to be briefed, pretended to know something about it, made suggestions for improvement, confirmed the special funds, left and forgot about the special research staff.

## II

Had anyone asked N. Nikofeyev whether he possessed any *intellectual arrogance*, he would have said no. He possessed emotional or genital arrogance. He was pleased to know he had trusted people in positions where they could barter deals with competent 'companions', to read his name in international specialist books, but, essentially, he only wanted one thing: to do as much research as possible and in as uncensored a way as possible.

Better than children, one reproduces oneself via MEMES, via knowledge that reproduces itself. Outside, the era of Gorbachev was passing, you could see it on TV. Nikofeyev described its spectral fade as 'a kind of provisional chaos' (chaos, always conceived as infinite, can never be of a provisional nature because it does not look ahead).

## III

In one of the grandiose, poorly managed swimming-pool complexes that remains from the empire in decline, built on the ground plan of a Tsarist cathedral, there is one forgotten basin that serves a special purpose. The women of a neighbouring tractor factory bathe there, like in a hidden spring that waters a pond. During the

BIG     SAVINGS, the abolition of the lifeguard's post was overlooked in parliament, and so a forgotten employee lived there, looking after this 'spring', the special pool, changing the water and so on. It has a constant temperature of 18°C in both winter and summer. Through the wide windows, the sun casts its blessed rays onto the surface of the water, whose movement is reflected on the vaulted ceiling.

Mondays, the forgotten lifeguard has the day off. That is the day N. Nikofeyev goes and follows an idiosyncratic drive: he swims himself out, and once the tiredness takes hold of his soul, he settles down in his body, expands completely, so to speak, entrusts himself to the water of the lagoon and lets his testicles and member be sprayed by the renewing jet of water that lies about 50 cm below the surface. For a moment he daydreams. Without much need for additional willing, his seed flows into the blue water (the bottom of the pool is a *dark turquoise*). He hopes that these tiny, flagellated, very robust messengers will be picked up by one of the many swimmers from the neighbouring tractor factory. This is how he thinks he can procreate in a *modern* way. He would not, however, consider this 'plan'—which might indeed surprise one of the swimmers—to be diabolical; his impulse is not 'blessedly old school' but, like modern science, fluid. Compared to an ancient satyr, 'unbound'.

## IV

What, as far as soul is concerned, is archaic? What is a *progressive* soul? Has it been sanded down?

At a congress in Cincinnati, N. Nikofeyev was sitting next to his completely besotted friend M. Popolov. A waiting period is a gestational period. They had the impression they would not experience anything there that they didn't already know.

The key phrase for archaic is: 'I don't trust myself.' The opposite pole, which leads out of a waiting period, is called: *sapere aude* (dare to know). You can do that without any arrogance. The friends did not believe in the 'unstoppable rise of genetic manipulation', as no consistent daring (= independence) can be based on such.[26]

## V

In summer Nikofeyev had cloned the so-called dwarves in his secret laboratories. He could trust his personnel's sworn secrecy. The first 'human computers' were twins, one attractive female and one male child. Nikofeyev surgically eliminated the procreative capacity of these beings because his knowledge told him he could not allow this life to have a will of its own, for he still followed Darwin's theorem that a second evolution would necessarily put an end to the first: our own.

The laboratories were in a patch of forest that had once contained barracks for the German Wehrmacht. Those barracks had been extended and given cellars. Nikofeyev's 'beloved children', designated in Roman crudity with a Latin number in the order of their 'birth', were still in their test tubes. To activate them would require implanting them in a human transmitter. These transmitters ('altered humans') would have to be registered with the residents' registration office in accordance with the law. This 'non-scientific problem' was, at the time, insoluble. And so the 'many souls' remained in their tubes.

---

[26] It is not the changing of the human being, but the creation of 'another being next to the human being' that leads out of the holding pattern.

## VI

A visit from Popolov. Nikofeyev had attempted to keep his results a secret from his friend the geneticist. Nevertheless, his friend had managed to find him despite all the Belarussian confusion. Popolov says:

- You could bring a few of the glasses over the Pamir route to Afghanistan. The exact same way the MATERIAL makes its way west, just in the other direction.
- And then?
- You insert the 'living souls' into Pakistani girls, who are for sale.
- And they make their way back along the opium road? With papers?
- To Tajikistan, then through the Fann mountains to Bishkek, to Manas International Airport, and from there to Marseille.
- Passports?
- Fabricated.
- But they are indeed machines.
- Obedient machines.
- That's the problem.

Nikofeyev did business against his will. His conscience told him that that kind of secret knowledge, the kind that gives you power, could not be exercised in pairs. All the same, he risked the pact with Popolov. Just so as not to be alone.

## VII

Years later, the corpses of Nikofeyev and Popolov were found on a pile of rocks outside of Marseille. Roving packs of dogs had torn the bodies to shreds. The dogs were shot.

The police in Marseille found no clues regarding the murderers' identities. Presumably, the organizations had grown tired of the 'cross-border transport' of the two wisdom keepers and tried to appropriate the business with 'modern slaves' (not particularly lucrative, given the need for secrecy). The Marseille organizations, however—if they were indeed behind the murders—had merely pre-empted those 'living souls' which harboured a tendency to turn against the human race and hence their two guardians.[27]

BIRTHING A SECOND EVOLUTION (over the previous year, Nikofeyev and Popolov had found a way to avoid 'resolution') was a dangerous VENTURE. It was cheaper to buy minors from their guardians, train them and transport them internationally. This is how the experienced criminals of Marseille saw it. It's still not the right time for the emergence of the devil of second evolution. Devils have a waiting period.

---

[27] Similar to the selfish gene, which destroys everything around it that inhibits its reproduction. Accordingly, without Nikofeyev and Popolov knowing a way to outwit them, the MEMEs built into the genomes are exclusively intent on driving out foreign memes. They possess murderous tendencies.

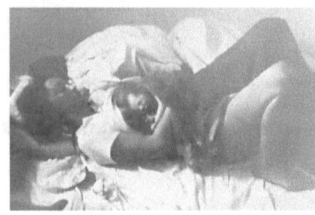

FIGURE 23. 'There is a mother, in whose body one has sat for 9 months, without a care, warm and in complete joy.' *Groddeck*, p. 6.

## THE UNDERWATER ARTIST

Bound hand and foot, he jumped off the Belle Isle Bridge into the icy Detroit River. He hit the hole he had dug in the ice perfectly. But the current dragged him away from it under the ice sheet. Thanks to the minimal space between the sheet and the water surface, however, he was able to catch his breath. The boundary between the aggregate states of water and ice is never exact. So the river guards were surprised when, a few kilometres downstream, he knocked on the thin surface of the ice. Like a ghost, he could be seen beneath the blank sheet, his nose pressed tightly against its undersurface to secure the few decilitres of available oxygen.

You can go to any point on earth, even those most unfriendly to life, said the artist after his rescue, by extending a spiral from your own centre.

## MODERN HUMANKIND

### RUMOURS OF THE SWALLOWED WORLD

Modern humankind has 'drunk the seas dry, unchained the earth from the sun, there is no longer anything existing that it has not imagined, i.e. made into an image'. Difficult to translate, Dr J. Vogl says. Already the word 'neuzeitlich'—what we are calling *modern* here—has no equivalent in French. The Gauls count time differently. For French counters, what comes before François Rabelais, before Montaigne, is not the unthinking period of the Middle Ages but Antiquity.

### RUMOURS OF ASSIMILATED THINGS

The swallowed world does not remain calm. It duplicates. It waits outside as an obstacle, as a trap, as a human object, and rotates inside as a stream of images.

Will a tin labourer in Siam or a boy in Mexico City be taken by this modernism to the same degree as someone living in the US or in Europe? Do they divide the world into images and treasures, they who are themselves conquerors who only hesitate for a moment? Without a doubt, Dr Vogl responds. And the billions of Chinese of different generations, six, twelve, eighteen generations back (and perhaps the future ones too, who act as spirits)—do they anchor HISTORY when they are characterized less by the modern era of the West than by CHINESE PARALLELITY?

For the moment, our ignorance in this regard will be the anchor that stops the all-out war of all against all for possession of the images, Dr Vogl says.

So you assume that large masses of inertia and perseverance, but of strength of character from earlier times too, I asked, exert an effect on us at a great distance and by skipping over time (similar to gravitation)? And that this holds the human earth together? A kind of inertia, based on people not yet structured by the NEW ECONOMY and modern times?

Dr Vogl looked pained, he saw the problem of translating such thoughts into French, which, thanks to its grammar, had clear rules against ambiguity. Whole armies of the dead are out and about, I continued, continuing to breathe in the manner of earlier ages, including the SWALLOWERS drinking the seas dry, the ones who have incorporated the earth into themselves and unchained themselves from the sun. They swallow themselves up and do not suffocate immediately only because this unfortunate state exists as a global average for only a fraction of a second, the old world of the giant Ymir still continues to act as inertia and puts the confusion into perspective.

It is unbelievably stressful, this back and forth, and cannot be compared to the curse of the flood whatsoever, Dr Vogl replied. You must believe me when I say that I have difficulty making such superimpositions clear in the context of the Bauhaus-Universität Weimar, and even more so in their translation into French, when the thoughts arrive in the polyphonic metropolis of Paris.

I see, I reply.

## SLAVE WATER

In the basements of the private genetic-engineering research institute Hilferding GmbH in Heidelberg, F. Kattebeer followed a simple assumption: the water which makes up close to 90 per cent of the human body is of a particular nature. It is old water and organized in such a way that it can only be transmitted by genes. It is therefore futile, he says, to carry out EXPERIMENTS ON THE RACIAL AMELIORATION OF GENTYPICAL STANDARDS if present-day water, e.g. tap water or water from the Rhine, is used in these experiments. And not just thanks to microscopic contamination. No. These are fluids that we and animals carry around in our bodies for our entire lives, sacred waters that have been sanctified by being passed down from generation to generation, primordial waters that are most closely approximated by the water from lakes hidden deep beneath the Libyan desert. Kattebeer obtained a vial of water from the underground seas that underlie North Africa's soil and immediately obtained a series of astonishing results in vitro. The cells responded to the water with 'almost fanatical fervour'.

Thus, in just a little time, Kattebeer will be capable of developing a short-stemmed, pain-insensitive, selectively (i.e. not comprehensively) intelligent hybrid human species. He had these rudimentary processes patented in the US. The new standard variety starts just below the definition of the human. As a result, they will not possess any human rights. The first specimens are to be grown on farms in the CIS, in freedom until the time of their taming and training. Kattebeer had been advised that there was a market.

## A LIFT INTO THE OCEANIC DEPTHS

Wilhelm D. Zabel, whose forebears are from Odessa, has enriched oceanography with a discovery. For years he has been the prophet of DEEP-SEA-TUBES, the OCEAN PUMP THAT ENCIRCLES THE PLANET, THE FUNNEL-LIKE STRUCTURE, i.e. all vertical structures of the water masses that characterize the blue planet. They are diverse due to the countermovement of their current, and the fact that cold undercurrents carry the warm surface currents like a rider. Confronted by the resistance of a coast or an underwater mountain range, these water masses change direction unexpectedly and force the countercurrent.

Some of the ocean's REVOLUTIONS are destructive, others create life. The bit of news that Zabel, too, is excitedly publicizing is the *Lift of Life*. Attached to the remains of wood and whale carcasses are masses of protozoa and bacteria, which sink from the surface of the sea into the depths at the unimaginably slow rate of 12 metres per year, thoroughly and constantly. There, close to the bottom, they remain for a long time and transform into creatures unknown to the world. Until now, researchers did not suspect life at these depths. Later, unicellular organisms, bacteria and their hosts rise again in one of the oceanic chimneys and 'forget' all the properties they acquired in the depths. This is the sense in which nature is secretive, Zabel says, she does not reveal the speed at which her metamorphoses take place; you just have to give her a great amount of time!

What we are dealing with here are 11 unknown species of micro-organisms that specialise in consuming organic matter. As far as bacteria are concerned, they are able to break down fat cold. They only do this in the depths, however, in the BALLET OF THE AEONS (they need 300 years to descend completely, stay at the base of the lift, specialize there and rise again in 60 years). The detergent industry is directly interested in this ability of theirs to break down fat. There is no way around Zabel if the industry wants to study the chimney effects of the oceans. They have to donate and act as sponsors.

Nevertheless, isolating the minimal existences is difficult. You do not catch things in the depths of the sea with a quiver. Zabel himself has never seen the creatures that are his namesake. He can, however, simulate them on his institute's computers according to the research data and 'bring them to life'. He has acquired patent EP 0695-351 B1 on the basis of such electronic demonstrations. Nature, Zabel says, is our navigator. It is from her we learn what it is we want to seek. The search itself does not take place in the inhospitable funnels where ships perish, but in sunny offices where business negotiations can be successfully conducted. I myself, Zabel says, can't even swim.

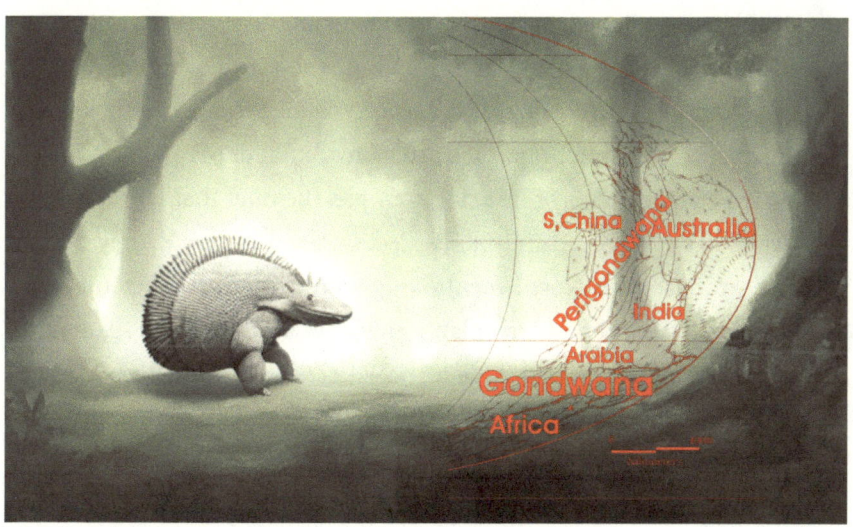

FIGURE 24. A lift into evolution: 70 million years before our time.

# HEINER MÜLLER AND PROJECT SPRING WATER

## THE POETIC MEANS COLLECTING

It was the week following Heiner Müller's return from Verdun. He longed for a bowl of porridge. Which wasn't served in canteens or pubs back then. And so he came up with a plan: he would hole up in a spa hotel in Baden-Baden. Maybe they would have some of the easily digestible oats. It had to do with hearsay. He couldn't sleep at night; he was tired throughout the day.[28]

During one of the long waits the poet spent in the luxurious hotel lobby, he was approached by a man whose name he thought he recognized from the academic holding patterns of the new federal states. Initially, he thought the man was insane. Mainly because the man was interested in their working together. The playwright was supposed to found a company with him—a technician, scientist and businessman—and offer his support through the production of poetic texts. Profits, the man said, would be shared.

He was in Baden-Baden, the man explained, because its underground cisterns still held water from the nineteenth century, water that Dostoevsky had enjoyed on his visits to the town. Nevertheless, the quality was disappointing, hardly any different than today. The buried canal systems of Iraq, for example, the ones that Dr Ing. H. Grapp had researched and catalogued, on the other hand, they still held secrets. Also worth mentioning were the deep-water tubes between Svalbard and Greenland, invisibly hidden in the sea but with great density. $H_2O$-20 is a special case. He had determined this from documents from the Academy of Sciences of the Soviet Union, but also from the laboratories of the Economic Office in the Reich Security Main Office (RSHA); for the rest, the reports

---

28 This was in November. Heiner Müller died 30 December.

had been archived by State Security. The collection included a complete list of all underground waters in Bohemia and Moravia with special documentation of their qualities, flow direction, oscillation and even various healing properties, 620 pages in total.

The rating scale ranges between 1 and 12. Was Müller following him? Müller nodded. Nevertheless, he had to wait. Water with a rating number of 12, the businessman continued, is considered priceless. Because of certain layers of stone, it emerges here on earth in only three or five places, e.g. in Pamir, where it's difficult to remove, as such water changes during transportation. Now the man introduced himself, gave Müller his business card. Prof. Dr F. Wilde.

In the provisional state-towards-death in which the playwright found himself, a person's personal defences against the willpower of others are not particularly pronounced. There was nothing that the playwright did not listen to that he did not 'let happen'. Indeed, at his core, this 'man of unshakeable calm' (from which he fed; at times when physical food is missing, the metaphysical takes its place) possessed a residual POWER OF IMAGINATION. He had never been a businessman and had no intention of becoming one in the short amount of time he had left. As it turned out, however, the former GDR researcher who'd been expelled from his office was keeping a state secret (largely without authorization and in the utmost secrecy). The secret had to do with some extremely rare water, a collection of samples in tiny test tubes. One single department of the extinct state had collected the treasure. Prof. Dr F. Wilde, who had belonged to its collectors, had assumed ownership of the abandoned property.

The ancient seas of the Sahara. There are 12. They are 66 million years old. Only in the Biskra oasis is there a cave which gives access to one of them. The entrance was sealed shut by order of the Afrika

Korps in 1943, before the British took Libya. The water samples contained unknown creatures. The water had a 'bloodlike taste' and quenched the average drinker's thirst 23 per cent more quickly and fully than that DIN-regulated standardized distillate we call drinking water. Were it possible to 'lift' these lakes by sinking a concrete mass under the lakebed (at a depth of 21 kilometres)—which shields the lakebed from the mobile mantle and presses the lake close to the ground—the water could be pumped. If it remains below the surface of the Sahara, it will not become salty. This kind of water supply would change the climate of North Africa back to the conditions of the prehistoric TETHYS OCEAN. One of the Axis' projects, planned for 1952. Researched by GDR hydraulic engineers in 1972. Presumably the reason behind Politburo member Lambertz's helicopter crash. Classified.

They didn't get to the founding of the joint venture. The playwright, however, had completely changed his mind about the odd man. In Wilde, examining the rarity of something as basic as water, he saw a poetic colleague. He would be happy to support the project with a few verses. They stayed in the lobby until 5 in the morning.

If the poetic is a process of collection like that of a hunt for berries and herbs, then the quality of the poetic shows itself in the tenacity, completeness, doggedness and passion that accompanies the search. It has to do with a complete or almost-complete collecting of oneself. A rough sketch of it, in a hand that is difficult to decipher, is Müller's final work.

The Reversal of Time's Arrow / 6:22 Min

Time Tumbles from the Stars. Triptych. / 1:50 Min.
(See p. 134 below)

**Film stills from:** *Von den Sternen stürzt die Zeit* (Time Tumbles from the Stars). Triptych. 'For Heiner Müller'.

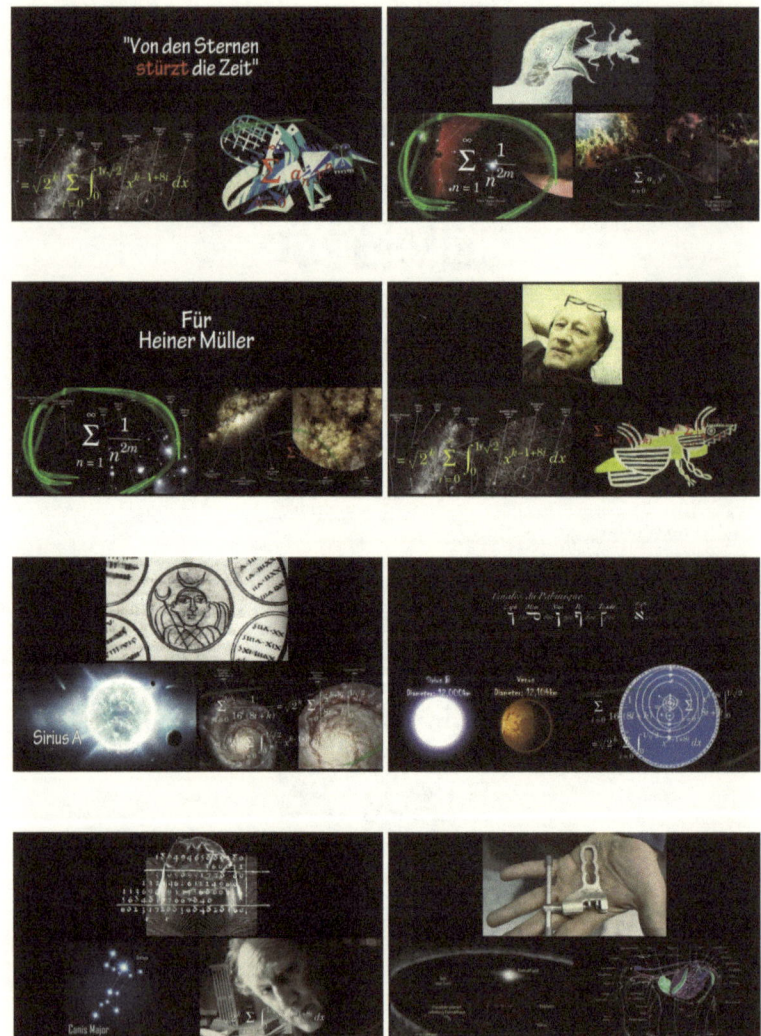

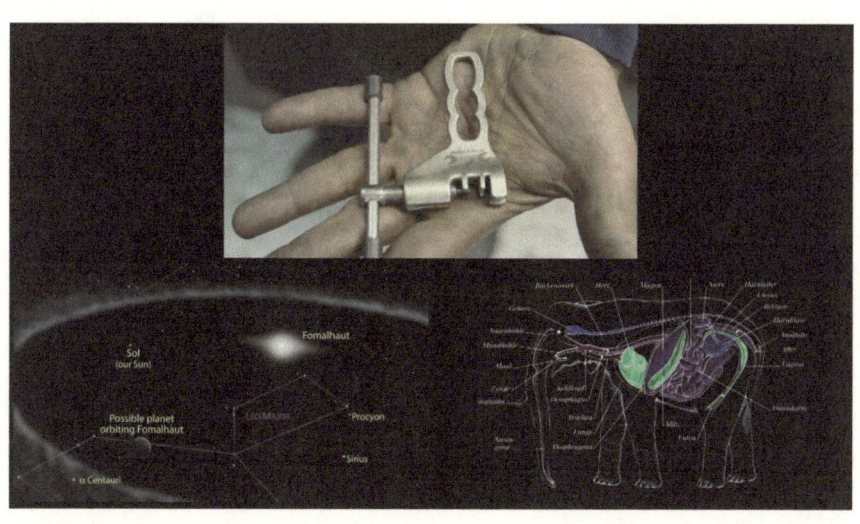

> 'Time from the stars rains down'
>
> Sophocles